Some other books from Norvik Press

Sigbjørn Obstfelder: *A Priest's Diary* (translated by James McFarlane)
Hjalmar Söderberg: *Short stories* (translated by Carl Lofmark)
Annegret Heitmann (ed.): *No Man's Land. An Anthology of Modern Danish Women's Literature*
P C Jersild: *A Living Soul* (translated by Rika Lesser)
Sara Lidman: *Naboth's Stone* (translated by Joan Tate)
Selma Lagerlöf: *The Löwensköld Ring* (translated by Linda Schenck)
Villy Sørensen: *Harmless Tales* (translated by Paula Hostrup-Jessen)
Camilla Collett: *The District Governor's Daughters* (translated by Kirsten Seaver)
Jens Bjørneboe: *The Sharks* (translated by Esther Greenleaf Mürer)
Jørgen-Frantz Jacobsen: *Barbara* (translated by George Johnston)
Janet Garton & Henning Sehmsdorf (eds. and trans.): *New Norwegian Plays* (by Peder W.Cappelen, Edvard Hoem, Cecilie Løveid and Bjørg Vik)
Gunilla Anderman (ed.): *New Swedish Plays* (by Ingmar Bergman, Stig Larsson, Lars Norén and Agneta Pleijel)
Kjell Askildsen: *A Sudden Liberating Thought* (translated by Sverre Lyngstad)
Svend Åge Madsen: *Days with Diam* (translated by W. Glyn Jones)
Christopher Moseley (ed.) *From Baltic Shores*

The logo of Norvik Press is based on a drawing by Egil Bakka (University of Bergen) of a Viking ornament in gold, paper thin, with impressed figures (size 16x21mm). It was found in 1897 at Hauge, Klepp, Rogaland, and is now in the collection of the Historisk museum, University of Bergen (inv.no. 5392). It depicts a love scene, possibly (according to Magnus Olsen) between the fertility god Freyr and the maiden Gerðr; the large penannular brooch of the man's cloak dates the work as being most likely 10th century.

Cover illustration: Photograph of the Heimaey eruption (1973) by Rafn Hafnfjörd.

CALLED HOME

by

AGNAR THORDARSON

Translated by Robert Kellogg

Norvik Press
1995

Original title : *Kallaður Heim* (1983) © Agnar Thordarson.
© Robert Kellog 1995: English translation of Agnar Thordarson, *Called Home*.
Cover photograph © Rafn Hafnfjörd 1995

British Library Cataloguing in Publication Data

Thordarson, Agnar
Called Home. — (Norvik Press Series B)
   I. Title II. Kellogg, Robert III. Series
   839.693 [F]
ISBN 1-870041-28-3

First published in 1995 by Norvik Press, University of East Anglia, Norwich, NR4 7TJ, England.
Managing Editors: James McFarlane and Janet Garton.

Norvik Press has been established with financial support from the University of East Anglia, the Danish Ministry for Cultural Affairs, The Norwegian Cultural Department, and the Swedish Institute. Publication of this volume has been made possible by a grant from the Icelandic Society of Authors.

Printed in Great Britain by Page Bros (Norwich) Ltd., Norwich.

Introduction

In the early morning hours of 23 February 1973, the 5,200 inhabitants of Westman Islands, a fishing village on the small island of Heimaey off the south coast of Iceland, were awakened from their first sleep with the rumble and thunder of a major volcanic eruption taking place near a farm called Kirkjubær, about 1000 metres from the centre of town. What followed was the remarkable story which forms the background of this novel by Agnar Thordarson. In one of the book's few departures from the historical record, a character is killed in the lava. In actuality, no lives were lost, either in the evacuation of the island, which began within minutes of the first explosions in the mid-winter darkness, or in the heroic effort to save the town's fishing harbour, the most important one in Iceland, by pumping cold sea water on the encroaching lava. This ingenious method of cooling molten lava, invented during the Heimaey eruption, has since made its way into the volcano textbooks.

When the eruption began, the first thing that occurred to many people must have been the memory of another historic eruption only ten years earlier. In 1963 a whole new island began to rise out of the ocean southwest of Heimaey. It was called Surtsey ('Surtr's Island') after the ancient fire giant who old poems predict will participate in the final destruction of the gods. Less poetically, the new volcano that appeared on Heimaey in 1973 has been called Eldfell ('Fire Mountain'). Its rough bulk now joins the more shapely Helgafell ('Holy Mountain') about a kilometre away, which has not been an active volcano for five thousand years.

Somewhat confusingly to the stranger, the town on Heimaey and the archipelago of small volcanic islands of which Surtsey and Heimaey form a part are both called *Vestmannaeyjar* (literally, 'Westmen's Islands'), which by convention has been Anglicized as *Westman Islands*. This name has since the Middle Ages been associated with a band of 'Westmen,' from Ireland or the western isles off the coast of Scotland, who sought refuge there from the Icelandic mainland during a slave revolt. Except for Heimaey, these islands are geologically recent and are uninhabited. In the summer, the Westman Islanders graze sheep on them and gather eggs from their cliffs.

Iceland sits at the northern end of a rift in the floor of the Atlantic Ocean, along which the continents of Europe and North America have for eons been gradually pulling apart. Consequently, it experiences the perturbations of a geologically 'young' land. Volcanoes, earthquakes, and eruptions of steam and hot water have conditioned the lives and the history of the people of Iceland, beginning with its settlement by Scandinavian and Celtic émigrés in the ninth century. The names of active volcanoes such as Hekla and Katla are a feature of every Icelander's consciousness. The most massive eruption of lava ever witnessed on earth in historic times occurred in southern Iceland in 1783 when almost 3 cubic miles of lava poured out of a series of craters along a fissure in the mountain Laki. These so-called Skaftáreldar ('Skaft River Fires') are remembered by a preacher in *Called Home*, who cites with approval the allegorical interpretation of them by the Reverend Jón Steingrímsson, at whose church door in a place called Klaustur the lava finally came to a stop.

The eruption on Heimaey is not the only historical event to which *Called Home* alludes with some precision. Its people are particularly aware of the Vietnam War, the American military presence in Iceland (the 'Defense Force' at the NATO base in Keflavik), the 'Cod War,' taking place at that time between Icelandic and British trawlers on disputed fishing grounds around Iceland, and the radical student movement and drug culture that had grown up in both Europe and America in the late sixties and early seventies. These larger international events serve as a reminder that, remote as in some ways their country is, Icelanders have always been drawn outward into a wider and more cosmopolitan world. Today this impulse is acted upon by a well educated and prosperous population of 260,000 people who participate in the intellectual and artistic life of Europe and America to an extent far out of proportion to their number.

In the Middle Ages some Icelanders journeyed as far from home as Constantinople, where they served in the emperors' Varangian Guard. Many of them left home for a longer or shorter time to serve the kings of Norway and to visit the Scandinavian courts in the British Isles. Icelanders were the major book producers of Scandinavia and wrote not only about their voyages to North America but about pilgrimages to Rome and Jerusalem. Making his way as a courtier or a viking abroad was an essential element of the aristocratic Icelander's education. Such foreign service was a source of honour, wealth, and worldly distinction. But in the ambiguous vision of the medieval family sagas, these same cultural forces are also seen as a threat to national and individual integrity. Something of that ancient unresolved love-hate relationship with the world beyond Iceland may be a permanent feature of the national character. It is implicit in the various senses in which Andri and the other characters of this novel are 'called home' from abroad, a trope that begins with the name of the place, Heimaey ('Home Island').

Agnar Thordarson, the author of *Called Home*, was born in Reykjavik in 1917. He and his sister and five brothers grew up at Kleppur, a mental hospital on the outskirts of the city, where his father, the distinguished physician Thordar Sveinsson, was director. Agnar's mother, Ellen Kaaber Sveinsson, was Danish, a fact which together with the father's learning in languages and science produced a cosmopolitan family atmosphere, even by Icelandic standards. Readers of W. H. Auden and Louis MacNeice's *Letters from Iceland* may recall that it was in this household at Kleppur that the young English poets were guests.

Agnar graduated from the Menntaskóli in Reykjavik in 1937 and began graduate study at the University of Iceland. He was a summer student at Oxford in 1940, and later during World War II he worked for the British news service in Iceland and the Ministry of Information and the BBC in London. He received his Master's degree in Icelandic Studies from the University of Iceland in 1945. The next several years were spent partly working as a librarian at the National Library of Iceland and partly travelling and attending lectures at Oxford, Paris, and Nice. He worked full-time at the Library from 1953 until his retirement in 1987, with occasional periods of leave for foreign study (Yale School of Drama, 1960-61) and lecturing abroad. He is married, with three sons and seven grandchildren.

In Iceland Agnar is perhaps best known as a playwright. More than thirty plays have been performed on the stage in Reykjavik, on Icelandic radio, or on television. He is the author of a collection of short stories (*Sáð í sandinn*, 'Sown in the Sand,' 1988), a travel book (about Icelandic writers visiting the Soviet Union), and five novels, the most recent of which, *Stefnumótið* (*The Appointment*), is a spy novel published in

1989. *Kallaður Heim* (*Called Home*) was Agnar Thordarson's fourth novel and was published in 1983. Three of his works have already been published in English translation. Paul Schach translated the novel *Ef sverð þitt er stutt* (1953) as *The Sword* in 1970, Einar Haugen's translation of the play *Kjarnorka og kvenhylli* (1953) as *Atoms and Madams* was published in 1968, and Robert Cook published a translation of his third novel, *Hjartað í borði* (1968), as *A Medal of Distinction* in 1984.

The story of *Called Home* is told in a way that reminds us of the author's mastery of dramatic technique. It is presented either as conversation or as the free indirect discourse of a narrator whose style and point of view are determined by the character with whom at the moment he is concerned. There is nothing of the epistemological complexity of modernist fictions that create a narrative which is itself the centre of its own story. Instead, the telling of this story has the immediacy and objectivity of a stage play, with a steadily focused, slightly comic and satiric, fictional world continually before our mind's eye.

These are characteristic effects of Agnar's fiction, a character-centred realism that accepts the world of Icelandic society pretty much as it finds it, while at the same time acknowledging its diversity of perspectives and values so as to make room for a gentle comic irony in the interplay among them. Realism of this sort tends to be conservative. It depends for its effect on a broadly shared knowledge of society and sympathy with its central values. It is rational and pragmatic rather than visionary, sentimental, or heroic. While these qualities of Agnar's fiction are related to the historical precision of his setting, they are not put to the exclusive service of scientific or photographic realism, in part because the world in which his characters live is not one that adheres unfailingly to the causes and effects of a conventional modern reality, no matter how straight-forwardly their story appears to be told.

There is room in it for some of them to converse with ghosts and for the traditional plots of romance to exert themselves against the claims of logic or probability. In this, as in so many other respects, Agnar Thordarson's art is true to the life of modern Iceland.

ICELAND

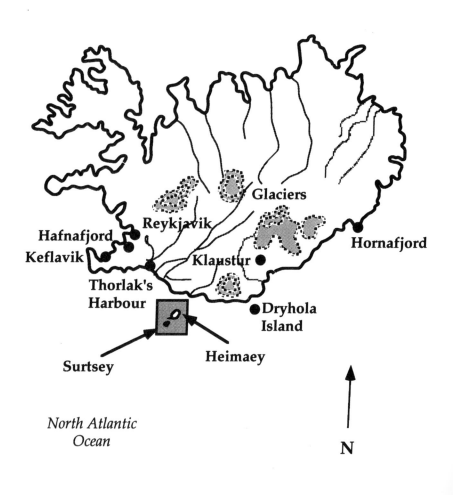

Glaciers

Reykjavik

Hafnafjord

Keflavik

Klaustur

Hornafjord

Thorlak's
Harbour

Surtsey

Heimaey

Dryhola
Island

*North Atlantic
Ocean*

N

Miles

0   100

0   Kilometers   150

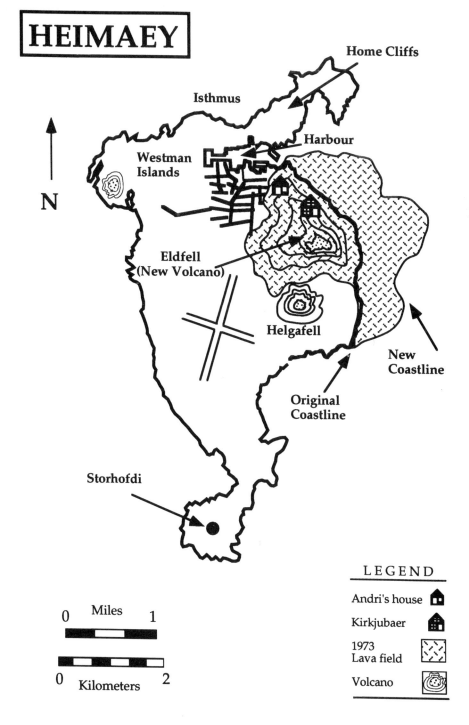

HEIMAEY

Home Cliffs

Isthmus

Harbour

N

Westman
Islands

Eldfell
(New Volcano)

Helgafell

New
Coastline

Original
Coastline

Storhofdi

Miles	
0	1

Kilometers	
0	2

LEGEND

Andri's house

Kirkjubaer

1973
Lava field

Volcano

I

Andri remembered exactly how the weather had been the day Howard ducked quickly through the door of the bookstore, shaking the rain from his hat.

'It's miserable weather,' said Howard, continuing to shake off the rain water.

'The low-pressure systems keep coming as if they were on a conveyor belt in the freezing plant.' Playfulness flashed in the heavily bearded face of the lighthouse keeper.

Howard pulled out a white handkerchief and wiped his face. He had a neatly trimmed light-red moustache and cheeks reddened by the weather, somewhat British.

'How many knots was the wind on Storhofdi this morning?' he asked.

'Oh, I suppose about the usual fifty-sixty,' answered Grimur the lighthouse keeper.

'But not down here in town.'

'Oh no, you don't take the town into account up there where we are.'

Grimur chuckled. He too had a moustache, chestnut brown and full, with a light streak in the middle from tobacco stains.

'We're a part of the ocean up there,' he added.

Howard had begun looking at the magazines and books on the shelves and in the racks.

'There's *Time* magazine. They didn't have it at the other bookstore.'

He began to leaf through it.

'Ordinarily we don't sell many copies of it here,' said Andri, 'but some people hope there will be something in it about our fight with the British.'

'I doubt that Americans are interested in the Cod War. They have enough going on in their own.'

'Who knows but something historic might happen in the fishing grounds any moment now,' said Grimur and rubbed his chin.

'Do you think so?'

'It feels as if something's in the air to me,' Grimur answered.

'Hopefully, though, people will try to keep their heads.' Howard handed the magazine to Andri, who put it in a bag.

'I don't remember this bookstore from the year I spent here,' he said, 'but of course that was a long time ago.'

'Mama started it some years ago,' Andri answered and handed him his change.

Howard put the magazine under his coat.

'And there's enough business for both of them?'

'Yes, I suppose they'll get by, but I am here only part time and don't have any interest in this kind of a shop.'

Andri indicated the toys, miniature cars, dolls and plastic merchandise of every sort, ship models and more that was on the shelves and counters.

'And the Danish magazines are still as popular as they were in the old days?' asked Howard as he buttoned his coat up to the neck.

'Yes, the women here couldn't live without them. We get them sent regularly from the Booksellers' Association in Reykjavik.'

'Provided the planes are flying,' inserted Grimur.

Howard nodded to them. He was ready to head back out into the weather.

They watched as he trudged against the bursts of rain that were moving across the town and turned the corner at the end of the street, where the masts of the fishing boats along the wharves came into view and the freezing plants stood.

'It's probably a shock to him being here in storm and rain,' said Grimur the lighthouse keeper. He had pulled out a large red bandanna and was ready to blow his nose.

'Oh, it's not always sunny in America,' Andri answered.

He jogged the magazines together that Howard had taken out of the rack.

'Yes, the gunpowder smoke from Vietnam probably drifts over the sun there sometimes.'

Grimur held the handkerchief with his thumb against one nostril and blew through the other with a great snort.

*

Several weeks passed and it wasn't until the shortest days of winter that Howard next came to the shop. Andri and his mother were waiting on people because the Danish magazines had just arrived and Christmas shopping was beginning.

Howard nodded to Andri as he entered the shop.

'I had completely forgotten how beautiful the sunset can be during these short days.'

It was dead calm and the orange-yellow daylight still glowed on the ocean surface.

'On days like this it is quite tolerable to be here,' Andri agreed.

'Here's just the book that I need to get,' said Howard, taking from the rack the new book by Gligorich on the chess match between Fischer and Spassky for the world championship.

'Were you in Reykjavik when their match took place?' asked Andri.

'Yes, I had just arrived in the country, but I didn't have the time to go to the hall and watch it. I played a little chess in the old days, but didn't keep it up in America.'

Fru Solveig had finished waiting on a customer and came

17

over to them now, smiling.

'This is my mother,' said Andri.

'Yes, of course, the bookseller herself.'

Howard bowed and they shook hands.

'Naturally you don't remember me,' she said and smiled. Her hair was freshly done and her red lips glistened.

'Of course I do, but I wasn't sure that you remembered me.'

'Yes, I always think of you on a bicycle, wearing white sneakers. It was unusual back then to see people riding a bike.' She laughed, and a gold filling gleamed in one of her front teeth.

'That was the summer before I graduated.'

'You lived in the Consul's house.'

'Yes, the Consul was my uncle.'

'And you often carried binoculars.'

'I wanted to be an ornithologist.'

'But then you gave up birds?' Solveig narrowed her eyes archly.

'They were a different kind of birds that I began to work with.'

'Wasn't that about the time,' she asked, 'that Frimann went to America?'

'Yes, he went two years before.'

Howard handed Andri the chess book.

'I want to buy this,' he said.

'And so you took over from Frimann in America when he came back home,' said Solveig, observing Howard closely, as if seeking some hidden movement in the features of his face.

'Yes, I took over as director of sales in Boston.'

'And now you are taking over from him again back here,' Solveig continued.

Some girls had come into the shop, and Andri went to wait on them while his mother recalled old times with Howard.

Howard looked over the postcards that were in a rack on the

counter.

'Frimann was rarely in the Consul's house in the last years.'

'So I understand.'

Howard had chosen several cards.

'His wife certainly couldn't think of being here after their son was killed,' said Solveig sighing.

Andri was still helping the girls.

'I remember that day so clearly,' Solveig went on after a short pause.

'It was such a bright and beautiful autumn day.' She took a deep breath.

Howard held the cards in his hand.

'There had been a fine rain that night and the grass was a little slippery. Puffin hunting had begun and Rikki always carried his gun for shooting birds.'

'He wasn't shooting birds that time,' her son broke in.

The girls he had been waiting on had left the shop.

'He was netting puffins,' he added.

'But before that he had often been shooting birds,' she retorted.

'But not that time, he didn't have his rifle with him.'

'In any case. He slid forward in the wet grass off the edge of the cliff. They couldn't get his body except by boat. It lay among the boulders at the foot of the cliff all bloody and mutilated. It was such a long fall. That day will never leave my memory, it was such a great shock to everyone in town.'

'It was a terrible accident,' Howard agreed.

'Fru Camilla has never really been the same after that,' said Solveig.

'They stopped living in the Consul's house and I think Fru Camilla has never come here since,' she added.

'No, probably not.'

Howard handed her the cards he had picked out. One of them was of the harbour with Heimaklettur in the background.

19

Another had a picture of Helgafell and the town below in bright sunshine, with green yards and blue sea and some fishing ships in the harbour. Solveig put the postcards in a white envelope.

'So you provide the populace here with spiritual food,' said Howard smiling as he took the envelope.

'This isn't the store that I dreamed of having, and sometimes I've thought of moving to Reykjavik, but nothing has ever come of that. I began with this bookstore shortly after my husband died.'

'I see.'

'He was the first mate on the *Wish II*, which the Consul owned.'

'I remember *The Wish*.'

'No that was *The Wish I*, this was *The Wish II*. The crew went to get her newly built from Bergen, and we wives got to go with our husbands. The trip was great fun, with a beautiful entry into the harbour inside the skerries in gleaming sunshine. But it was fated that they would lose her in the surf on the sands.'

'That has been the graveyard of many ships,' said Howard. He put the envelope in his pocket.

'Three of them made it to land,' she whispered sadly.

'My husband wouldn't leave his shipmate who had injured a leg, and tried to get him to the shipwreck shelter which he knew was no more than a few kilometres from where they had gone aground. The third man headed in the direction of town to get help. He lost his way in the snow storm and didn't appear until the next day, more dead than alive.'

'And your husband?' Howard asked in a low voice.

'He would have made it to the shipwreck shelter if he hadn't thought more about saving his shipmate than about himself. They found them both frozen to death when the storm let up, not far from the shelter. Yes, it sometimes costs everything you have to be a hero. I was alone and helpless, with Andri a baby,

20

and if it hadn't been for the Consul's help I would have lost our house and not been able to support Andri later at school in Reykjavik.'

More people had come into the shop. Howard said goodbye and went back out into the midwinter twilight, which had become deep grey.

*

Andri was alone in the shop a few days later when his friend Kalli rushed in with a brown cardboard carton in his arms.

'It's good that I've found you alone,' said Kalli in his black Che Guevara beret, and set the box down on the counter in front of Andri.

'What do you have?' Andri asked.

'A lot of brochures about the territorial waters dispute and the Cod War and some pamphlets about the war in Vietnam.'

Kalli meanwhile emptied the carton. The brochures were in every colour, and he arranged them on the counter.

He started telling Andri about the fishing trip he went on with his brother Gubbi.

They had been drift-net fishing and lay a long way inside the fifty-mile limit. Before they knew it, one of the British trawlers which had been several miles in the distance all of a sudden headed at them, splashing as it came.

'My brother Gubbi grabbed the megaphone and called out of the window, but it had no effect, the Briton didn't turn at all, but headed straight at us. Gubbi managed at the last second to turn hard to starboard so that we just grazed the trawler with the bow, but the damned Grimsby peasants pelted us with all kinds of trash, machine bolts, cans, empty bottles and scrap iron. They pulverized the window in the wheelhouse.'

'What did you do?'

'We couldn't do anything. I told Gubbi that next time I'll

take my shotgun, and it's not hard to make hand grenades.'

'Didn't you take down the number of the trawler?'

'Of course we did, but what good do you think that was? They made another run at us, except that we were more on guard against them this time and they didn't get close enough to throw trash at us. They yelled at us and stuck their bare asses over the rail. It would have been fun then to have some buck shot to send them.'

'Couldn't you call the Icelandic patrol ships?'

'Yes, but they were a half-hour away, chasing other trawlers.'

'Of course they will be charged.'

'Charged, what do you think will come of that? No, the only thing they understand is bullets and bombs.'

'There are a lot of people in Britain now who are coming over to our side, both in the press and in Parliament.'

'I don't give a shit for that kind of blabber-mouthing. Haven't some people there been demanding that the British navy be sicked on our fishing fleet?'

'Our point of view is winning out. And yet a lot of people think that the British have some right to the fishing grounds, based on the fact that they have fished there for hundreds of years.'

'What you mean is they have stolen from us for hundreds of years.'

'There weren't any fishing limits then.'

'Is it the author of the famous poem about Vietnam who is talking like this?' said Kalli scowling.

'I don't see that it has anything to do with events in Vietnam.
. . .'

'Oh yes, it is exactly the same kind of struggle for freedom against imperialism, and you ought to know that. I am here with a supply of pamphlets and brochures to display in your window.'

'I don't think Mama will agree to that,' Andri answered calmly.

'Your Mother! You aren't still tied to her apron strings, a famous poet.'

'If you think that you can insult me by calling me poet with every word it won't work.'

'Stop pretending, you obviously have something to say about running the shop.'

'No, I am only here part time, as you know. My mother owns it herself and runs it entirely without my interference.'

'Come off it, man, you can get your own way whenever you want to. I know that much from when you used to trick her out of money for films that were banned to children. . . .'

Kalli laughed, and they put some brochures out into the window.

As might be expected, Solveig was not slow to notice the pamphlets in the middle of her displays when she came back to the shop.

'Who put that junk out in the window?' she asked angrily.

'They are booklets about our dispute with the British over the fifty-mile fishing limit. . . .'

'It's nothing but Communist garbage, which I will not have among beautiful books and fine Christmas gifts. Take them out at once. I know that Kalli brought them to you – I saw him just now.'

'Mama, I'm not here in your shop to let myself be ordered about like a dog – in that case I'll leave,' Andri answered bluntly.

Solveig burst out: 'Kalli is always your evil spirit, this Communist mouthpiece who is too lazy to do an honest day's work and lives like a parasite in filthy communes in Copenhagen or Amsterdam where they are supported at the expense of the taxpayers.'

'He is entitled to his ideas without interference from you and

23

other bourgeois.'

'Yes, just call me a bourgeois – I'm not ashamed of that.' She went out into the window and picked up all of the pamphlets.

'It could ruin Christmas sales to have that kind of trash on display among beautiful things.'

They argued for a little while, with the result that Andri got to keep the pamphlets behind the counter, where they were less objectionable.

'I think Kalli would be better off remembering that if your father had thought less about saving his father's life I wouldn't have had to be a widow with a little boy.'

'How do you know he doesn't?'

'No, he always acts as if we should feel indebted to him – – and I know that on many occasions he has told you all kinds of lies and dirt about me. He thinks that's the right way to repay me for everything I've done for him.'

*

As in previous years, Solveig invited Thorkell, the secretary of the city council, to take her to the party given on Twelfth Day by the Women's Auxiliary of the rescue squad.

When they danced, he swung her so vigorously that she was afraid her upswept hair would escape from its fastening, and when he wanted to pull her up close to him she held him away at a more suitable distance.

Spotlights illuminated the dancers so that sometimes they looked dusky brown, while at others they were bathed in a yellow brightness that made them look seasick.

Solveig breathed easier when the set was finished and she had escaped from the arms of her partner.

She walked toward their table. The black dress, with dazzling gold Egyptian designs printed on it, fit tightly across full hips that were beginning to lose their firmness.

They were settled at their table again when her eyes landed on Howard, the plant manager, in the doorway.

She waved to him cheerfully and motioned for him to come over to them.

'Why did you do that?' asked Thorkell coldly.

'Because he seemed so lonely there.'

'A man like that shouldn't have any problem getting a woman for himself.'

'I'm not sure he would go to the trouble for just anyone.'

'Don't they say that he had an affair with Frimann's widow in Reykjavik?'

'You are so full of mean-spirited gossip,' whispered Solveig through clenched teeth, for by then Howard had come to their table.

Thorkell stood up and invited him to sit with them.

'Do you know each other?' asked Solveig.

'I know at least that he is about the most powerful man in town,' answered Howard smiling and sat down with them.

Thorkell called to the waitress who was bringing refreshments to the next table.

'Cognac and coke, right away.'

'Are you here by yourself?' Solveig asked after he was seated.

'Yes, I thought I would drop in for a few minutes to support the cause.'

'The old Consul used to come here all the time,' said Solveig, 'but I don't think I ever saw Frimann here after he came back from America.'

'His wife didn't dare let him out,' Thorkell interjected, but Solveig ignored the remark.

In a few minutes the waitress returned with coke bottles, cognac and glasses. But the ice at their table had melted.

'You ought to see to it that the manager of Isborg has enough ice with his drink,' Thorkell said in a playful tone. The waitress took the water pitcher from the table and hurried off to get some ice.

Thorkell asked the manager about operations at the freezing plant while they waited for the ice.

'Most of the work to improve the cleaning positions for the seasonal employees has been finished,' Howard said, 'so the girls will have tall chairs to sit on. It was intolerable that they had to stand all the time.'

'I remember how hard I found it sometimes bending over to salt with my father in the yard at home.'

'Are you expecting many party girls from Australia this winter?' asked Thorkell smiling broadly so that the short broken teeth in his lower gum showed.

'You are assuming they will be party girls,' said Howard.

'Not on my account,' answered Thorkell, 'more on someone else's perhaps.'

The waitress came back with the pitcher full of ice.

'That's good,' said Thorkell. 'The plant manager needs a whole ice palace when he is getting ready for action.'

Thorkell poured their drinks and they raised their glasses.

'I have actually heard that many of these girls come from very good homes in Australia,' said Solveig. 'They come to Europe just to see the Old World.'

'And set up practice maybe now and then,' said Thorkell and laughed.

Solveig immediately asked Howard to dance with her and he looked inquiringly at Thorkell.

'Certainly, by all means, dance.'

Solveig moved her hands down over her hips as she stood up from the table, and the Egyptian designs glistened in the black material.

'I don't want to make Thorkell jealous,' said Howard when they had moved out on the floor.

'He has nothing to say about what I do,' she whispered and pressed herself close to the plant manager. She knew that the expensive scent of Chanel Number Five would have a good effect, and she hoped not to be in the yellowish green light if he looked at her while they danced.

'There is also no reason he should, because I don't know how to jitterbug the way I saw you doing before,' said Howard.

'Ah, I never really get in step with Keli,' she whispered, 'and I have no idea where he learned to do those steps.' They moved away from the band because the sound was too loud for them to hear each other.

'I don't remember anything about Thorkell from before,' he said after a short pause.

'No, it hasn't been many years since Keli came to the Islands. Did you hear that he was made mayor the year the president came on an official visit?' But Howard had not heard the story.

'He came home a little tight from Ollerup the chemist's birthday party and was half undressed when he suddenly remembered the president's visit the next day. So he went back outside with the flag and began to raise it up the pole – but in his hurry he had forgotten to put on his pants – so there he stood in his underwear in the bright summer night hoisting the flag. . . .'

'Did anyone see him?'

'Of course, poor Keli was never made mayor again. Everyone laughed at him.'

The dance was over, and when they came back to the table Thorkell had disappeared.

'I would be very glad if he could find someone else to jitterbug with,' she said as they sat down.

The people at the next table were watching them.

'Look how they are whispering about us over there,' she said, touching his arm. 'There doesn't need to be anything more sometimes to start gossip about a person in such a little town.'

'I think it would do more damage to your reputation than mine,' Howard answered playfully.

'Oh, no, it makes no difference at all what is said about me. There was a lot of gossip about Frimann and me in the old days – maybe you've heard some of it?' But Howard denied knowing anything about it.

'Tell me how it happens that a man like you should come here,' she asked.

'Isn't it good to be here?'

'Oh sure, it may be all right for those of us who aren't used to anything else, but it's not that way for a man like you.'

'It's an interesting life here – human and ornithological.'

'Aren't there enough birds in America?'

'Not my kind of birds. I remember when I was here in the autumn at the Consul's that I sometimes helped the kids who had found unfledged puffin chicks get them over to the Isthmus.'

'Oh, yes,' Solveig answered, 'that happens every autumn – they often fly onto the street lights in the dark.'

On the crowded dance floor Thorkell could be seen swinging a small woman in a wild dance.

'What kind of bird do I remind you of?' whispered Solveig. He contemplated her, with her diadem, dangling earrings, golden chains and sparkling gems.

'Oh, I think a bird of the hummingbird family,' he said.

'I'm glad it wasn't some kind of sea bird, a puffin or black guillemot.'

'They are very colourful.'

'But I am sure you did not remember me well when you came into the shop right before Christmas.'

'Yes I did.'

'I always remember you with binoculars, and it wasn't only birds that you were looking at.'

Her black nail polish glistened as she took a cigarette from the pack on the table.

'Well I didn't need binoculars to notice you talking to the Danish chemist in the chemist's shop,' said Howard playfully.

'Oh, you've heard gossip about him and me?'

'No, I don't think so.'

'Yes, I know you have, and it isn't true – there wasn't anything between us – he just couldn't leave me alone. He tricked me into accepting a pair of sunglasses from him, which I never should have done.'

'But I do think I heard something about you and Frimann, if I remember correctly.'

'Yes, that could be, and I can't deny that I was attracted to Frimann for a time. I went up to his room in the attic of the Consul's house in those years and listened to jazz records with him. Old Ella always gave me the evil eye when she saw me on the stairs.'

'The old woman watched over her people very carefully.'

'Like a witch in the fairy tales. Do you remember the song, 'On the Sunny Side of the Street'?'

'With Louis Armstrong?'

'Right, with him – Frimann played it so often for me then, and it has reminded me of him ever since. If a person could only be on the sunny side of life.'

Howard lit the cigarette lighter. She took his hand as she drew the flame into the cigarette. From her gold bracelet dangled small golden elephants.

'You remind me a little of Frimann as he was then,' she continued.

She looked at him and batted her long black artificial lashes, like little tassels.

The melancholy notes of the saxophone came to them. She looked downward with an expression of sadness.

'What did Frimann die of?' she asked after a some moments of silence.

'Of a heart attack.'

There was another silence between them. The painful sound of the saxophone grieved for nights in the past.

'Yes, his heart,' she said softly. 'He didn't treat it very well.'

'Apparently not.'

'Nor other people's either,' she added.

Sounds echoed from Armstrong's time: Night and day, you are the one. . . .

'Don't you think that Frimann sometimes got homesick,' she asked cautiously, 'in America?'

'Maybe, but Frimann was not the kind of man that would ever let it show.'

'And yourself?'

'There is always something amusing happening everywhere, the trick is just to get a look at it.'

'And have you done that here?'

'Yes, I have just begun to see.'

'Do you know how Frimann met this Mexican wife of his?'

'She's not Mexican, except on one side – she was born and raised in the United States.'

'But she looks like a Mexican squaw.'

'She is a striking woman.'

'Do you think so?'

'Haven't you met her?'

'Me? No, she wouldn't associate with anyone here, except the people in the Consul's house. People here weren't fine enough for her – I've only seen her at a distance, and it seemed to me that she was awfully tense and nervous, her face so drawn.'

Just then Thorkell came up to them, dripping with sweat, from the dancing.

'What an impressive couple you and Villa make,' said Solveig, not without a touch of sarcasm, when he sat down with them at the table.

'I thought I'd never get away from her,' Thorkell answered, and drank what was left in his glass at a single gulp.

'That's because you took such deep dips with her,' said Solveig teasingly.

Thorkell motioned the waitress to pour a shot of cognac into his glass.

'There's another thing I'd like to ask the plant manager about,' said Thorkell when he had taken a sip of his drink.

'Oh Keli, don't change the subject – we were a long way into our conversation.'

'Yes, I saw you rubbing up against each other,' he answered roughly.

'How vulgar you can be!' Solveig complained.

'You are welcome to ask me anything you want to,' said Howard amicably.

'It's a question that many people here in the Islands are eager to know more about.'

'Please go ahead.'

'It came to many people as a surprise that my friend Julius, a supervisor at Isborg for many years, should not be made manager when Frimann died.'

'Maybe he will be later on,' said Howard calmly.

'You know very well they sent a telegram to Howard in Boston about taking over the position,' Solveig shot out at Thorkell.

'How should I have known that – from the lady maybe?'

'Try not to be funny – everybody here was talking about it,' Solveig glowered. 'You don't need to act as if you didn't know a thing.'

'Of course I know, like everyone else,' said Howard calmly, 'that Julius has for a long time been Frimann's right-hand man.'

'Especially after Frimann moved to Reykjavik,' said Thorkell, without allowing the hatred in Solveig's glance to have an effect on him.

'But Julius isn't an engineer like Howard,' Solveig objected.

'Julius has the kind of education that does you the most good in life.'

'He never went to any school,' Solveig retorted.

'He went to the school of life right here, and it's a better education than any school in America can give.'

'Julius is excellent – I value him very highly,' said Howard calmly.

'That's exactly why I was asking. . . .'

'Shouldn't we quick-freeze this subject for the moment,' Howard continued, and poured plain coke into his glass.

'Oh just take another turn with your little Villa, Keli, she's always glancing over at you. She wants another dip.'

'You obviously think the plant manager is a free man, Solla dear,' said Thorkell smiling broadly.

'Well, aren't I?' Howard asked in a rising tone of interrogation. 'Or does higher authority intend perhaps. . . ?'

'There is another authority besides higher authority,' Thorkell answered, 'and maybe no less powerful, though maybe it would be better to call it lower authority in a certain sense.'

'You're always talking in some kind of riddles that no one understands, Keli.'

'Oh the manager won't have any difficulty understanding it, you either, Solla, because everyone here knows full well what power is was that determined the outcome of this decision.'

'Everyone knows that the directors of the company sit in Reykjavik,' Solveig said glowering, 'and all decisions are made there, in the meetings of the directors, and nowhere else.'

'Has Fru Camilla perhaps confided this to you. . . ?'

At the same moment the dance music started again with a loud blast, so that all conversation was drowned in the din.

They sat and watched people stand up from their tables and blend into the crowd in the middle of the floor.

Soon after, Howard thanked them and left.

'This is the last time that I come to a dance with you, Keli,' Solveig said when Howard had left the table.

'We'll see about that,' he answered and ran his hand along her thigh under the table, although she tried to get away from him.

*

Andri stayed up late into the night writing a poem about the Cod War that had been struggling for a long time to find expression. Now he wanted finally to write it, but one draft after another came to rest in the wastebasket.

The preceding month he had often turned over in his mind how he could approach such a subject to give it a fresh and original appearance, so that it might produce an epiphany in the minds of his readers, opening new and unaccustomed vistas to them. He had written poems which at first he was thoroughly pleased with, but when the transport of ecstasy had passed, and they had lain in his drawer for several days, had proved to be inane jingles – more of a kind with the poetry of Grimur the lighthouse keeper than with those liberating words he sought and claimed to be frightened of in his own poetry.

In itself he was not opposed to the poetry of Grimur the lighthouse keeper, which relied on old fundamentals of national poetic tradition, but it could not be the model for a developing young poet of high ambition, who wished to take untrodden ways to a reality that manifested itself to mankind through some new image.

The Vietnam poem that had made him famous in certain circles in the capital he had composed in a great frenzy all one night, and not a word needed to be changed when it was printed. People immediately memorized it and recited it in coffee houses, meetings, and student parties. He had put the obscure feelings of people's hearts into words, but now, when he was in an even better position to write, knowing all the events of the Cod War in every detail, and having, besides, the eye-witness accounts of people like Kalli and other seamen from recent clashes, it was as if the words did not have the strength to support themselves.

It was not unlikely that the proximity of the events made it more difficult for him to see them in a dramatic light – describing them did not result in the powerful imagery he had been able to produce in the famous Vietnam poem.

Kalli thought it ought to be a simple matter for a recognized war poet to shape the words of an inspired satire that the nation would absorb and learn by heart about British aggression against Icelandic fishermen in their own fishing grounds. But when in actuality the images appeared in some ways overwrought and untrue, they would have had less effect than as if Grimur had written a poem in his manner. With elaborately constructed imagery in a conventional style Grimur always reached a certain audience that was able to appreciate such poetry. But Andri knew that his readers would expect something altogether different from him and would reject him as an important contemporary poet if he did not produce something that was lively and illuminating at the same time.

Why in the world was he less successful in describing actions that he knew thoroughly than those which in reality he knew very little about and had no personal knowledge of, such as the war in Vietnam?

And ever since he wrote the famous poem the suspicion had grown in him that he had over-simplified the matter. It would be more complex than being able to divide men into angels and devils – most people were something of a mixture of the two – simple explanations and simple solutions were to a greater or lesser extent false and unworthy of a serious poet – he would have to dive deeper if he were to come up with those pearls that he claimed for his poetry. In the war of liberation that he wanted to see in the fishing dispute with the British, it was absurd to

34

describe them as devils – he and his readers knew them too well for this – and thus it remained, the poem shapeless on his paper.

*

It had gone below freezing during the night and become icy when Solveig came out with her escort. Thorkell had developed an erratic gait, but it was not a long way home, and before they knew it they had come to the walkway that was illuminated by her outside houselight, on which ice needles glistened like falling stars in the peaceful night.

'Don't fall,' she whispered and went before him up the cement steps. The door was unlocked.

Thorkell came right behind her.

'Don't make any noise,' she whispered.

Thorkell pushed her ahead and muttered something under his breath.

'You don't deserve it at all for me to let you come in,' she said and turned abruptly to face him.

'Don't be stupid,' he said and pushed her ahead into the vestibule. He stretched over to the door handle and opened the door into the living room. They were greeted by the pent-up odour of upholstered furniture and foam rubber. He went to the middle of the floor and wriggled out of his overcoat, which he threw onto the sofa. His black turned-up hat went the same way. Solveig went back into the kitchen.

He unbuttoned his jacket and was loosening his tie when she came back in and spoke in a tone of reproach.

'And I had looked forward so much to going out tonight.'

'I'll make it up to you.' He undid the knot in his tie.

'Why are you doing that?' she asked.

'To get out of it as quick as I can.'

'I don't want you getting undressed down here in the living room,' she said sternly, 'and I won't have you throwing your coat and hat on the sofa.'

'Hang them up then.'

She took the coat and hat and went with them into the hallway, which was small and crowded and where there was a staircase up to the attic with a rounded handrail that was the first thing her son had slid on.

Thorkell took his vest and jacket off and hung each of them on the back of a chair. He leaned back on the sofa.

Solveig came back in and looked at him disapprovingly.

'You can't come near me.'

'Oh, we'll see about that,' Thorkell smiled broadly.

'I find you repulsive,' she said.

'It wouldn't take very long to get you to stop shivering,' he said grinning, and reached out for her, but she struck his hairy hand.

'I don't want you – you ought to go home – Andri may still be awake.'

'That hasn't bothered us before.'

'But you have produced such a revulsion in me.'

'You wanted the plant manager. I saw it in you tonight.'

'I wanted to talk with him about the old days,' she said and sat down on a chair by the table, out of his reach from the sofa.

'I wanted to talk to him about the Consul's house – I haven't been there in many years.'

'No, not since you stopped giving the old man his bath and letting him poke you with the scrub brush.'

'God, you can be an animal,' she responded.

Thorkell laughed maliciously on the sofa.

'It's very clear to me that you would rather see someone else here on your sofa, but I am here now in the flesh and even more ready for action when you whimper and carry on – it gives me such a challenge.'

'Do I have to call Andri?'

'You can for all I care – when we've started he can learn a lot.'

She jumped to her feet intending to go into the hallway – the bedrooms were up in the attic – but he seized her like a black panther in the doorway. She gave a low cry and struggled to get free.

'I'm not going to let you out of my grip,' he growled, half carrying her to his lair on the sofa. She fought silently, trying to pull his hair and scratch him, but he overwhelmed her with his weight and a few powerful holds. She cried faintly.

'Let me go, let me go, I don't want to.'

A whinnying sound came from him.

'Yes, you want it, I feel it, you want it. . . .'

He stroked her belly and the whinnying became friendly and seductive. He put his hand inside on her bare flesh.

'You'll tear my dress,' she grumbled.

'I will if you act so wild.'

'Don't do this,' she begged, 'Andri could walk in.'

But he paid no attention to her plea and continued to move his hands over her. 'Not here,' she asked, 'let's go upstairs instead.'

'Now that's more like it,' he said, and raised her up on the sofa.

She stood up and pulled down her dress, which had been pushed up around her and rumpled.

'You can never behave like a civilized man,' she said.

'It all depends on you how I behave, and now I find that you are coming to your senses. . . .'

He had kicked off his shoes. There was a hole in the sock of one foot so that his toe showed.

'You went to the dance with a hole in your sock!' she said with disapproval.

'Because you haven't been doing your job,' he answered, and pointed with his fingers at how much the nails had grown.

'And I'm supposed to cut your nails?' she snorted.

'Well you wouldn't consider it too much to do if it was

another man's toes.' Thorkell smiled broadly.

'How stupidly jealous you are of Howard.'

'I saw how he was rubbing up against you.'

'That's not true.'

'Do you think I didn't see you? He is about to die for lack of a woman.'

'Now weren't you saying yourself this evening that he was having an affair with Frimann's widow?'

'Sure, but when she is not around he tries to meddle in other people's affairs, and I want to prevent it.' He began again to move his hands over her.

'I don't want that,' she said and tried to get loose.

'You're always best when I've worked you up against me first.'

'Don't you want some coffee?' she asked, having worked herself free.

'Is it made?'

'It's in the thermos in the kitchen.' She went back to get it.

Black hair showed through his unbuttoned shirt.

'How disgustingly hairy you are,' she said when she came back into the room.

'You have been able to appreciate it up to now.'

She poured the cups and they sat across from each other.

She watched with disapproval as Thorkell put four cubes of sugar into his coffee. He slurped it up.

'You ought to show Howard the poem that Andri wrote about Vietnam,' he said, and set the empty cup down away from him.

'What for?'

'Don't you think that Howard knows anything about poetry?'

'I think that has nothing to do with it. Andri kept bad company when he was at the University, which is why he quit medical school.'

'Yup, it's a pretty good poem, I can tell you, but you need

to know something about poetry to see it.'

'As if Andri had the slightest idea about what is really happening in Vietnam! Of course it is based on nothing but what these windbags have been harping on for months, even years at a time.'

'Yes, it was much better made than you would expect from a young poet. I have some faith in him.'

Thorkell smiled expansively at Solveig and made himself comfortable.

'Do you want more coffee?' she asked.

'No, I want you.'

'It will be for the last time tonight,' she said, and put the cups back on the tray.

'You should admit that you need to hold on to me as much as I do you – there is no inequality.'

She stood up and took the tray.

'Tax returns are due at the end of the month,' he said smiling.

She nodded.

'They're always giving reminders of it on television.'

She went back to the bathroom. Originally there had been only a toilet under the stairs, but she had it greatly enlarged by joining it to a little room off the kitchen that Andri had used and changing it into a fashionable modern bathroom, with pink and black tiles up to the middle of the wall all around.

She saw her plump pretty face in the ornate mirror. It was mostly free of wrinkles, but in some places bulged a bit from little deposits of fat.

She tried to smile at this pretty face in the mirror, but there was no anticipation in it, only resignation.

'You mustn't make any noise,' she whispered to Thorkell who had come into the entrance hall.

'Andri could be awake.'

Thorkell pointed to his feet, with the big toe sticking through the hole in one sock. In his stocking-feet he looked like a black bear walking on his hind legs.

They crept up the stairs. Thorkell could not refrain from taking her full hips in both his hands as they went up the creaking steps.

*

The town was not awake when Andri went out on a dark Sunday morning in the blackest short days of winter and walked down to the harbour.

On the wharf the lights hung gloomy and forlorn, scarcely lighting the boats that awaited the winter fishing season bound in thick ropes one to the other.

Toward the sea he saw a greyness over the islands to which as a child he had gone with his father, and come home with boxes full of guillemot and kittiwake eggs, tastier than other eggs. He recalled falling down in the boat and breaking some eggs. The yolks stuck to his sweater and hands. The natural-coloured sweater with a reindeer pattern had been stained from then on by the egg yolk, which his mother hadn't been able to get out.

Sometimes he imagined to himself that his father had not been shipwrecked but was on an egg trip instead, out on one of the islands and would come home unexpectedly with a large box full of speckled guillemot eggs.

He went along the wharf. It gradually brightened over the masts of the boats.

He spoke to Gubbi, Kalli's brother, who had had his boat put into a slip in order to change the engine before capelin season.

Gubbi was much more heavily built than Kalli, with a shorter neck, like a pillar of stone standing firm against the movement of the waves. They said he had a dream woman who told him where to fish, and he had been first in the capelin catch one season.

40

'Haven't the search ships left for the north?' asked Andri.

'It's way too far to sail north after them. We won't leave here before they begin to form up off the east coast.'

'Don't you think they could end up fishing them out like they did the herring?'

'No danger of that, they breed so fast,' Gubbi spit out brown tobacco remnants. He wore a blue sweater with a turtleneck up to the chin.

'Isn't Kalli coming with you?'

'No, Kalli – he isn't interested in anything but getting on a patrol boat to fight against the Brits.' Gubbi laughed and took some tobacco out of a plastic can. He offered the can to Andri, who declined it.

'When are you going to move into the new house?' asked Andri.

'I've moved. Didn't you know? Kalli helped me move before Christmas. You've got to come and see the mansion, man, drop into my bar and have a German beer.'

'I went up along there last autumn and saw that it was going to be really splendid.'

'What you see from the outside isn't half of it. Completely mechanical – kitchen and laundry more or less automatic . . .'

Andri went back up from the slip in the direction of the freezing plant. It was full daylight, although the sky was darkened by low clouds. Gulls swarmed over the harbour in search of food.

Andri was contemplating a flock of sea birds swimming in the mouth of the harbour when he heard a voice behind him. It was Howard, with his snap-brimmed hat and well trimmed moustache.

'It looks to me like some longtails are among them,' he said.

They studied the birds a few minutes and heard them calling out.

'Sure enough, that's the sound of the longtail,' said Howard.

41

'And that agitated *kurr-r-r* is the eider duck,' said Andri.

There were also other species of birds, black-backed gull, black guillemot and fulmar.

Howard invited Andri to come home with him and play some chess.

On the way to the Consul's house Howard told him that the prices of capelin meal and codliver oil were constantly rising on the world market, mainly from the fact that anchovy fishing by the Peruvians had completely failed during the same period.

'Isn't that caused by over-fishing, as with the herring?' asked Andri.

'No, fishing experts attribute it to changes in ocean currents along South America.'

They came to the Consul's house. It still hinted of the old stateliness, although it had obviously been poorly maintained.

In the Consul's time it seemed as if it was always freshly painted – white walls and red roof with overhanging eaves, a little in the Danish style, and balconies in the centre that made you expect elegantly dressed aristocrats would come out on them. But Andri had never seen anyone outside, not even the Consul's grandchildren when they visited, but the Consul had been visible, standing in the windows of the balcony doors or in the sitting room windows, with a telescope in his hand, when he was observing the ship traffic out of and into the harbour.

They went in through the gate that stood half open and partly broken away from the posts, with the pavement up to the house all more or less in pieces. In the area in front lay the flagpole, with patches of rot on it. Bare currant runners on which the Consul's wife had tried to grow berries for jam stood up against the house, sheltered from the north wind, but the whole garden had long ago fallen into neglect, so that the changes in seasons showed no effect. Frimann had obviously not cared about keeping up the house after his father died – and old Ella paid attention to nothing but what happened inside. The white walls had turned grey in the direction of the rain so that bare masonry was uncovered, and the paint around the window panes had in many places fallen off or flaked away, revealing unprotected wood. In the last years Frimann had kept only one foot here, otherwise living in Reykjavik.

Howard opened the heavy oak door, which plainly had not been oiled for many years and had begun to split and warp from the encroachment of the weather. They stepped into a vestibule laid with black and white floor tiles more like an office than a private home. There was a large coat rack with cattle horns, but one horn was cracked and seemed to be hanging loose. An old Bornholm clock reminded Andri that he had been here before, but the clock had stopped working and the face with the Roman numerals had grown dim.

The hands showed the time to be just before eleven, as if it had stopped when the Consul gave up the ghost. In this house time stood still. An oil painting of an old man greeted them as they entered the parlour.

'Have you ever come here before?' asked Howard.

'Yes, once or twice when my mother worked for the Consul.' He remembered clearly this painting of the old man in full regalia, but here in the painting he wasn't grey-haired, as Andri remembered his being, but dark-haired, with a brush cut, a little hedgehog-like, as in the caricatures of him in *The Mirror*. His uniform was dark blue with gold epaulets and buttons, orna-mentation on a high stand-up collar and a belt on which a ceremonial sabre was fastened. On a circular table was his Consul's hat with a white feather.

'I wonder why he didn't have his hat on,' asked Andri when he had contemplated the painting for a while.

'He probably wanted to be courteous to the painter by sitting bareheaded before him,' answered Howard, 'and it's also more personal.'

Howard went to the large glass cabinet that stood in the

43

corner.

'Of course the old man showed you his bird collection,' said Howard. 'He was very proud of it.'

Yes. Andri well remembered this unique collection of mounted birds: various species of gulls, auk, black guillemot, puffin, tern, oystercatcher, fulmar, and eider. Particularly, he had been fascinated as a child by a king eider that he had never seen before, with a peculiar knob on its bill that was like a diadem.

Back in one corner stood an old-fashioned seal gun, and on the walls shelves full of books, especially various kinds of spiritualist writings: many years of *Morning* in black leather bindings, books by Helgi Pjeturss about Icelanders on other planets, and writings in Danish about mysticism and life after death.

On the parlour floor lay a bear skin which Andri used to be halfway afraid of, with glistening fangs, black muzzle and the dangerous yellow-green eyes of a beast of prey.

Howard went to the handsomely carved three-legged chess table with chess men carved out of walrus tusk. Immediately they were absorbed in chess. After two games, which Howard lost, he proposed that they get themselves some refreshment. He went back into the dining room and called into a brass tube next to the dumb-waiter down to the cellar, where the kitchen was, the abode of Old Ella. This tube was like the ones formerly used by ship captains to call down from the bridge to the engine room.

Andri asked Howard how Old Ella was doing cooking for him.

'She's great at boiling haddock and smoked lamb,' said Howard and smiled. 'Other than that, I very often eat at the cafeteria down the street.'

They had not finished the third game when they heard the step of the old woman on the stairs. She dragged her feet as

44

though she were afraid of losing her shoes. Howard called to her.

'Ella, do you have anything in the coffee pot and something to go with it?'

She started when she saw who was there, and Andri stood up and greeted her with a handshake.

'You know Andri, don't you?'

She looked at him with water-blue eyes, but the expression in them was very vague. She murmured something in a low voice and drew her hand back as she greeted him.

'Would you like crullers with the coffee?' she asked after a moment's reflection.

'Yes, crullers,' Howard repeated after her, 'that would be excellent. You're a big cruller man, aren't you Andri?'

'Moderately.'

'Do you have anything else?'

'I have newly made meat paste.'

'Yes, maybe we should each have a slice of rye bread with meat paste. What do you say to that, Andri?'

'Sure, I think that would be great.'

'I also have whey-cheese,' said the old woman, awaiting a reaction.

'Whey-cheese? What do you say to whey-cheese, Andri?'

'Whey-cheese? No, I guess I'll pass it up.'

'Yes, we'll pass up the whey-cheese this time,' said Howard.

The old woman turned back to the dining room and from there down the stairs to her quarters.

'You probably recall Old Ella clearly?' said Howard when they heard her making her way down the stairs.

'She doesn't get out much, but I remember her well. You don't easily forget the way she looks at you.'

'Yes, she saw something around you.'

'Do you think so?'

Howard laughed. 'Sometimes she murmurs something to herself, and my interpretation is that she's talking to the Consul then.'

Andri had not heeded the danger his queen was in, and now Howard took her from him.

'I knew it! The old woman had a good reason for coming in.'

'For producing illusions on the chess board,' said Andri pretending to be angry.

'Old Ella stands by her people,' said Howard and laughed.

*

It had begun to grow dark again when Andri headed home from the Consul's house.

He was greeted by long-familiar cooking odours when he opened the entrance hall door.

Back in the kitchen his mother was flushed with colour over pots and pans.

'Where have you been?' she asked, and slid the potato slices into the brown pool of melted sugar in the pan.

'I was playing chess. Did you remember the red cabbage?'

Yes, she had remembered it and the strawberry jam, which was indispensable with the Sunday roast.

Andri told his mother where he had been.

His mother turned the heat off under the pan of crackling melted sugar.

'Did Howard ask about me at all?'

'About you? No, why?'

'He was at our table for awhile last night.'

Andri went into the living room and turned on the television.

'Is anything supposed to be on now?' she asked absently. She began to bring the food to the table.

The picture on the screen came into focus and an animated cartoon appeared.

46

Andri turned down the volume as the sound came on.

His mother took the leg of lamb out of the oven.

'He sat for a good while at our table.'

'Who?'

'Howard. We talked a lot about the old days.'

'Isn't he a lot younger than you?' Andri stood up and went to get a coke from the refrigerator.

'Do you want a coke?'

'Yes, I am so thirsty from the heat in the kitchen.'

She brought the gravy in and looked in the drawer for a gravy spoon.

'Yes, he's somewhat younger than I, but not much. He was here one summer before he graduated, with his uncle the Consul. I remember he always wore white sneakers, even though it was a very rainy summer, and usually carried binoculars. He was sure he wanted to be an ornithologist. But he was only a boy then, tall and lanky and nothing special, not a sophisticated man as he is now.'

She took off her apron and smoothed down her hair.

They sat down at the table.

'Isn't everything just the same in the Consul's house?' she asked when Andri had finished cutting them each a slice of lamb.

'You could say that everything's just going down hill. Where's the red cabbage?'

'I forgot to bring it in from the kitchen,' she said and stood up from the table. She returned with the cabbage in a bowl.

'Be careful. It's very hot.'

'What brand is it?' he asked as he took the bowl.

'Brand? The same us usual. . . .' She sat back down.

'Beauvais?'

'Yes, I did notice that.'

Andri took a thin slice of meat, put it in his mouth in one piece, and smacked his lips as he chewed.

47

'Is the roast good?' his mother asked.

'Exactly the way it should be.'

His mother smiled. These were their best moments.

Andri picked up the coke bottle and poured it into their glasses.

'I suppose she's turned ugly?'

'Who?'

'Fru Camilla.'

'I don't know anything about that.'

'Keli said that Howard was having an affair with her, which explains why he got the job after Frimann.'

'How does Keli know that?'

'I don't know, but she certainly did go to America from time to time, and she could have met Howard in Boston then.'

'There are a hundred million men in America,' said Andri and took a drink from his glass.

'She was always bored in Iceland.'

Andri continued to enjoy his roast without answering his mother.

'I think it was difficult for Frimann to be married to her through the years, and I am certain that could have played its part in his dying so suddenly.'

Andri said nothing, glancing at the television, but the cartoons were still on.

'We should invite Howard to have a roast with us,' she said after a moment's pause.

'Did you say Howard?' asked Andri.

'Yes, I mean, it's way too big a roast for the two of us.'

'We usually eat it cold afterwards.'

'And the cooking that Old Ella does. . . .'

'Smoked lamb or haddock, that's okay.'

'And I enjoy asking him so many things about the old days, and what it was like in America.'

Andri was looking at the picture in the black frame that hung on the wall across from him. He had often examined that picture carefully. It was the one picture in existence of his parents during their courtship. They had gone on a camping trip on the mainland, to Spring Lake. A young man with a low forehead and hair combed with water sat in front of a white tent in a clearing in the woods and held a laughing young girl by the waist. She had taken off her shirt, and her large white breasts filled out her brassiere.

It had been on Whitsunday, and his mother told him that a dust storm had been so thick that the mountains and Hekla weren't visible, and the woods barely leafed out because the spring had been so dry and cold.

'Didn't you have anything at Howard's?'

'Yes, Old Ella brought crullers and coffee.'

'How was she?'

'As usual, a little older and greyer-haired, her hands as stiff as wood. Howard said that she saw something ghostly surrounding me, but I know he was just teasing.'

'Pish, there's no reason to pay attention to what the old woman pretends to see. The Consul believed in her enormously, and she knew how to play on that, but I am certain that more than half of it was nothing but fakery to make herself interesting in his eyes.'

'Didn't they say she warned Frimann that something unexpected could happen to the child?'

'Yes, you did hear something like that.'

'And Frimann connected that with automobile traffic, which is why he wanted to be mostly here in the Islands where there wasn't any traffic.'

'I don't think this story started circulating until after Rikki fell.'

Andri took another sliver of meat.

'I also need to apologize to Howard,' said his mother after a moment's deliberation.

49

'Apologize? What for?'

'Keli acted so badly toward him last night.'

'It's not the first time that man didn't know how to behave.'

'But I was to a certain extent to blame. I unintentionally made him a little jealous.'

'You should break it off with this man.'

His mother looked at him in surprise.

'I really thought you got along pretty well with Keli. You've sometimes talked to him about books.'

'That's entirely different.'

'He talked a lot about your poem last night.'

'Really?'

'He praised it highly. And whatever might be said about Keli, he knows a lot about poetry and owns a great many books. He said that you were the most promising of the young poets.'

She would have liked to continue the conversation, but her son signalled that the news was coming on, and at that moment a picture appeared on the screen of an Icelandic patrol boat sparring with a British trawler. The crew of the patrol boat had succeeded in manoeuvring their notorious scissors across the trawl-wire where the ship had been fishing by itself, unprotected by a British escort vessel.

The commentator told about an order from the Ministry of Naval Affairs in London to British trawler captains that they should stay together if they were fishing within the fifty mile limit. Only in that way could the escort vessels protect them against the treachery of Icelandic captains in their small but maneuverable patrol boats and the dangerous equipment they employed. An effort would be made to develop a weapon that might be effective against their infamous scissors.

Solveig looked anxiously at her son when the commentator had finished reading the announcement from Her Majesty's Ministry of Naval Affairs.

'What kind of weapon do the British want to bring to the

fishing grounds?'

'I don't know, but all they understand are bullets and bombs.'

'You don't mean, though, that we should arm the men on our patrol boats?'

'Of course. In war it's impossible to avoid shedding blood.'

'And how do you think it might end?'

Andri laughed.

'We are invincible because we are so small. The media will see to that.'

She stood up and began to clear the table.

The news continued on the television.

A picture came on of Nixon, who had ordered an end to all air attacks on North Vietnam. Kissinger, his representative at a peace conference in Paris was seen walking with Le Duc Tho, the chief representative of the North Vietnamese. They walked inside a high chain-link fence.

The commentator said that it would probably not be long before all hostilities were ended in Vietnam and a permanent peace established. Free elections would then be allowed to proceed, a more democratic government be established, and then at last the people would be able to live in friendship and harmony in this productive land, enjoying freedom and security against oppression and fear.

Solveig had finished clearing the table.

'I think that it will be all over between Keli and me,' she said and looked searchingly at her son.

'I wouldn't mind that,' answered Andri without meeting her gaze.

*

The winter fishing season was about to begin and people streamed in from everywhere. Even from Australia and New Zealand came girls who had been travelling in Europe and heard

51

of lucrative jobs far north in the Polar Sea.

They had hired themselves out to work in the freezing plant and were now taking up their quarters in the fishing huts.

It shocked them not to know a single word in the language of the natives, and the food they were supposed to eat they could scarcely touch to their lips. They lived mostly on canned food and crackers the first days.

They came into Andri's shop to ask about textbooks in this strange language so they could at least understand the foremen, but there was a poor selection of such books. Andri showed them children's books about outlaws and fairies which might possibly do, but it didn't seem to them that they would be any help in the freezing plant, and they ended up buying picture magazines.

Capelin boats were ready to put out from the harbour immediately, but the weather bureau warned of a deep low-pressure system moving fast from Labrador in the direction of Iceland.

'These continual low-pressure systems are getting the best of me,' Solveig complained to her son. 'I can't stand them.'

In addition to that, a dark-skinned Indian had come to town who went from house to house selling a British encyclopaedia in twenty-four volumes at a big discount, with a white bookcase included as part of the bargain.

The Indian explained to people in almost incomprehensible gibberish how it would be possible to acquire great erudition from these books.

'And the old ladies completely fall for it that a coal-black Indian tries to talk to them in their language,' sputtered Solveig.

Andri didn't respond.

'Oh yes, this could literally knock the legs out from under all a person's business. I will report him to the Booksellers' Association in Reykjavik.'

She flounced out of the shop, but the worst of the weather

had come.

She could foresee that weekend business was going down the drain – the Danish magazines wouldn't arrive from the Booksellers' Association until after the weekend. There could be no flying in such weather.

And that proved to be right. The violence of the weather increased, and no one went out of doors as the hurricane was passing over. But by Monday morning flights had resumed.

Solveig was coming out of the bookstore from having distributed the Danish magazines when she saw Howard at a distance.

He greeted her and thanked her for the other evening.

'Which way are you going?' she asked.

It was dead calm. The lights reflected off the smooth sea.

'I am coming from saying goodbye to some Japanese capelin buyers. They came here today to find out everything they could about processing it, and they were very exacting.'

'Wasn't the weather horrible over the weekend?' she asked.

'Yes, but it's no worse than you can expect this time of year.'

'Did it make a lot of noise in the Consul's house?'

'It certainly did. It howled and moaned like a piece of modern music,' said Howard laughing.

'In weather like this I just want to sleep and sleep. I really am allergic to these low-pressure systems from Labrador.'

They walked along the waterfront. The masts of the boats made a kind of forest, where they lay one outside the other from the pier. Men were seeing to their boats and getting ready to set out the next night for the fishing grounds.

A yellow glimmer of daylight was still out on the horizon.

'Don't you find it difficult to be without everything you're used to in big cities – theatres, concerts and all of that?' she asked after a moment's silence.

'Not at all. The sounds of the weather are my concerts now,

and there will be lots of drama among the birds in the spring.

'Always these birds.'

They had gone beyond the harbour. Sounds carried so well in the calm that they heard the shouts of some boys who had lit a bonfire out on the Isthmus. The flickering light was reflected off the smooth surface of the harbour.

'Do you plan to go somewhere over Easter?' she asked.

'I don't know whether I'll be able to.'

'Before this I was never able to travel over Easter. I was so tied down to the shop, but now I have Andri.'

'Will he be taking over the shop?'

'No, that hasn't been decided. I only got him to come because I wasn't feeling very well this autumn. But I could just as easily have had an impulse to sell it.'

They walked very slowly.

The boys' bonfire was quickly subsiding.

'The travel agents in Reykjavik have started advertising trips to the south of Spain and concert excursions to Vienna,' she said.

'I have travelled very little in Europe,' said Howard.

'I thought it was such fun to dance the Viennese waltz when I was a girl. . . .'

They heard a foot-step behind them and stopped for a moment.

Thorkell came out of the darkness.

'Keli, what are you doing here?' she called harshly.

'I've got to talk to you,' he said breathlessly.

'Are you running after me for that?'

'I saw you through the window, and I hadn't found you before. . . .'

'I'll talk with you later,' she said and turned away from him.

'I have called the Booksellers' Association about the Indian.'

'It can wait.'

'But there is something else that can't wait. I have to talk to

54

you about an urgent matter – privately.'

'No, I have nothing to discuss with you since your behaviour the other evening to Howard. It was contemptible.'

'I have forgotten it, if there was anything,' said Howard and moved away from them a little.

'I wasn't in a good mood,' stammered Thorkell.

'It was absolutely nothing at all,' answered Howard.

'I don't want you chasing me – I want you to leave me in peace,' said Solveig and stomped her feet. 'You have no rights over me.'

'No, I know that, but this can't wait.'

'I'm sorry that I am a little short of time,' said Howard, 'I'm expecting a phone call.'

'We'll see each other later,' Solveig called to him.

Howard heard her reproving Thorkell in a harsh voice.

'Why are you spying on me – I won't stand for it.'

'I had to tell you right away – I've been offered a job in Hafnafjordur, a very good job. . . .'

*

They sat in front of the television waiting for the commercials to be over.

'I went by the candy store and bought you some Linda chocolate,' said Andri and laid the bar in a blue wrapper on the table beside her.

'No, you shouldn't have done that, because I bought some Cadbury myself today. I've already had a bite. It's in my purse.'

'You shouldn't buy British chocolate when we are at war with them.'

'I thought I deserved it after being shut in all weekend.'

She stood up to get the handbag.

'I also ran into Howard.'

'Oh, yeah?'

'And then before I knew it Keli had come up beside me out

of the darkness. I have no peace from that man.'

'Didn't you say that you were going to ask him whether the Indian man had a right to sell books from house to house?'

'No, I don't need to. Everyone has that right. Do you want some Cadbury?'

She handed him the package.

Andri shook his head.

'He has been offered a job in Hafnafjordur,' she continued and sat down again in front of the television.

'The Indian?'

'Stop it! – Keli of course.'

'Good for him.'

'A very good job.'

'Then he will doubtlessly go there.'

'He asked me to come with him.'

'To Hafnafjordur?'

'To get married.'

'Congratulations.'

'Would you like that?'

'It's none of my business.'

'Of course it's your business.'

'Did Keli kneel down and propose? It's hard to imagine that.

'He cried.'

'He cried? With joy?'

'I rejected him.'

Andri looked questioningly at his mother, who had found herself a piece of chocolate out of the package.

'Naturally, I grew tired some time ago of selling notebooks and pencils to kids, but. . . .'

'Don't you want to go to Hafnafjordur?'

'Yes, I have nothing against Hafnafjordur. On the contrary, I think it's a very charming town.'

'Then what?'

'I don't love him.'

56

'Do you think that matters so much – for a woman of your age?'

'I am still in the bloom of life. Many men like a mature woman better than a young girl. I can see that very clearly from the way some of them look at me.'

She was a bit warm in the cheeks.

Her son grew thoughtful, but didn't say a word. On the television there were reminders to file tax returns on time.

'I think I have every right to enjoy life,' she said with a look of determination at her son.

'And that would give you the opportunity to associate with all the foremost people in Hafnafjordur, I mean the people who count for most. . . .'

'No, I couldn't let myself say yes, even though to a certain extent I half wanted to. But I don't love him. And who knows but I might still meet a man that I could love for the rest of my life?'

She had taken another piece of Cadbury, and licked the corners of her mouth with her slender tongue like a starving wolf in a fairy tale.

'No, you definitely won't if you keep on gobbling up chocolate. You're getting way too fat, and no man wants to take a second look at you.'

'Not at all, I'm watching myself. . . .'

The picture on television began.

A car was seen travelling in bright sunshine on a winding mountain road, where the driver made the curves by only a hair's breadth. It was none other than the famous Saint.

*

Howard sat at the desk of his uncle, the old Consul, and leaned back in the Consul's chair. He ran his hand along its arms, which were pleasant to the touch, the grain of the wood

57

having grown more conspicuous through the passage of the years. The threads of the screw-in feet had not begun to wear despite their age.

It had been a busy day: first the arrival of the Japanese, and then the complaints of the Australian girls that they weren't able to eat Icelandic food, and his assurance that they would soon get used to fresh haddock and cod. It was aristocratic food and very expensive, not often found in even the finest restaurants in the world.

The union secretary had surveyed the accommodations and sanitary facilities for the temporary workers and expressed satisfaction with the changes. Howard had also made a study of all the price increases of the past year that resulted from the latest devaluation, especially oil, fishing equipment, electricity, harbour fees, and every kind of repair work. He had compared the records of catches with last year's records, when cod had arrived in the fishing grounds earlier than this year. The boats' hauls now consisted for the most part of pollack, ling, haddock and red sea perch, but cod was rapidly increasing.

The fleet had lain in the harbour because of the weather over the weekend. Starting around midnight they intended to set out for the fishing grounds, the capelin boats to the east of Horna-fjordur, where scouting ships had spotted significant schools of capelin forming.

Howard leaned back in the chair with the seamen's almanac in his hand and pondered the outlook. The moon was auspicious, as was the whole prospect of a large catch in the days ahead, if the weather didn't ruin it.

He went back to the dining room and called down the speaking tube to Old Ella and asked whether she had any coffee, and was no more disappointed than the day before.

At this time in the evening he often listened to the news broadcast of the B.B.C. World Service. The announcer said that President Nixon would address his people within a few hours,

58

and it was expected that he would proclaim the end of the war in Vietnam and a treaty of peace.

Howard had taken his coffee and crullers from the dumb-waiter and was about to turn off the dining room lights when all of a sudden the crystal and china rattled in the hand-carved cabinet. Up on top of it was perched a stuffed falcon, its claws clinging to a black stone that rocked back and forth.

At the same moment there was a loud noise outside, and the inner door of the balcony opened of its own accord and started banging. It was just as though something frightful had walked through. The Consul suddenly came to Howard's mind, but was as quickly dismissed. The door should have been latched. He turned the key in the lock of the outer door, which was very stiff and opened out. It creaked on its unoiled hinges.

These doors were seldom opened. The climate did not invite picnics on the balcony. The old man may have permitted himself to dream of homage being paid to him on ceremonial occasions, perhaps on his fiftieth or sixtieth birthday, with a torch-light procession, but such affection never developed. The Consul was never popular and he had been hard to deal with in negotiations with the union.

Howard looked out over the low-lying town which lay sleeping in the dark winter night, yellow lights scattered here and there in the blackness. Down along the harbour the lights of the pier were reflected in the still sea. The spotlights on the front of the freezing plant shone on the boats that were readying themselves for fishing. It was still and calm, with a soft murmur of air.

Howard inhaled the cool air. The old midwinter month of Thorri was here, but the townspeople would not have much time in the next weeks for the singed sheeps' heads, pickled meats, blood puddings, animal bellies, ram testicles, and sausages of the Thorri feast.

He went back into the parlour and locked the door carefully

behind him. He was going to pour some coffee into his cup when the telephone resounded. Who could be calling so late? It would have to be something urgent, unless it was from the United States, where the day hadn't ended yet.

At the same moment, there was a roar in the air, as if from out of nowhere a jet had come in over the town. It occurred to him that the military command at Keflavik might be training pilots in attacking a Russian submarine in the pitch blackness.

He picked up the phone. It was the watchman at the freezing plant who shouted something unintelligible into the phone, a word that might have been *fire*, *fire*. Howard shouted back, asking whether the fire department had come.

In that instant he imagined the freezing plant in flames, with all the new equipment and carpentry work. Fresh in his memory were pictures in *Morgunbladid* of the freezing plant fire at Sutherness, which resulted in the loss of millions. Or had the fishermens' huts caught fire, where the girls were? Nothing would be more horrible than if one of them died in a fire while working for him. Then he could make out the word *volcano*. Howard put the receiver down. He was relieved. It was neither the girls nor the plant itself. At least he would be spared an official investigation. But there wasn't time for meditation. He slipped into the jacket he had hung on the back of the chair and hurried into the front hall.

When he came out into the darkness he could see a red glow over Helgafell. How could it be? That hadn't been an active volcano for many thousands of years. He ran down to the freezing plant in no time. People were running about, calling and shouting, and there was a heavy rumbling in the distance, as if the surf had greatly increased. All of a sudden, columns of fire shot up out of the mountain. He dashed into the freezing plant, where all the lights were on and everyone was in an uproar. Julius came up to him amazingly calmly. He told him that the Civil Defence headquarters in Reykjavik had been notified and that the greatest danger was that the mountain might explode in the next few minutes and molten lava flow down over the town. For this reason people had been told to get themselves as quickly as possible down to the harbour, where the fishing fleet would take them aboard and try to get out of the harbour in time.

*

On the television screen the Saint had succeeded at the last minute in saving the dream goddess from the villain's clutches and offered her a glass of champagne, as the halo appeared over his head.

'Oh, what an ordinary life a person lives,' Solveig sighed. At that moment appeared a picture of Lyndon Johnson, the former president of the United States. The announcer reported that a little while earlier the president had passed away on his ranch in Texas.

'I thought he had died a long time ago,' said Solveig.

'Yes, he really did in some ways. The Vietnam war did him in.' Andri remembered a caricature of the president shortly after he had had abdominal surgery, showing reporters in the hospital the scar from his operation, and in the drawing it had the same shape exactly as the map of Vietnam.

'How was it that the Americans couldn't win in Vietnam?' Solveig asked her son, as if she had completely forgotten the famous poem he had written.

'It was really because the media defeated them,' he said calmly.

'The media?'

'Yes, and it's the first time in the history of the world that the media alone have defeated a major power.'

He surprised himself with his answer and began to turn it over a little further in his mind. Could this be the subject for a sequence of poems – the power of the media over people's

61

minds?

He was deep in thought and his mother had just sneaked a piece of Cadbury chocolate when the house was jolted as if it had been struck by a loaded truck. The angel chimes in the window, which had been forgotten since Christmas, began to turn. The floating cherubs whirled with golden trumpets around the flashing Christmas star.

'What's that?' asked Solveig.

'Someone has driven a truck past here,' answered her son.

'This late?'

'Yes, working time and a half.'

A slight tremor followed.

'No, it's probably from the furnace. There were some kind of knocking sounds in it the other day.'

Andri went down to the cellar, from which noises were coming that he couldn't identify. He wanted to see whether they came from the pipes or the furnace itself or even from the tool room, but the door wouldn't open readily. It must somehow have been out of alignment with its hinges because it was always kept unlocked. And then he heard the din again, as if a tractor or a bulldozer were working outside, although it was an extremely unlikely time for such activity, even on overtime.

What could it be? He went out on the pavement and looked around. He heard a strange rush in the air, but there was nothing to see, black darkness, no stars anywhere, the moon hidden by thick clouds without a break anywhere. A dark and oppressive midwinter night. But the rushing sound from the shore, what did that mean? Maybe it came from the surf hitting the cliffs after the storm. Sometimes sounds carry a long way in calm weather when people are listening.

He heard footsteps on the gravel below, recognizing at the same time a familiar voice.

'What's going on?' called his neighbour.

'I don't know.'

'The weather couldn't be blowing up?' he wondered.

'It could be, I haven't looked at the barometer,' Andri answered.

'No, there wasn't anything in the weather forecast tonight, but these lows can move fast, without any weather report preceding them.'

'And the weather ships can be somewhere else.'

'I was walking my sister down the street,' the teacher said, 'when we heard the rumbling.'

'Yes, my mother and I noticed it, and then I heard a kind of droning down in the cellar.'

'There's an unusual current in the air now,' the teacher said. 'It would be a good idea to check the windows and doors carefully for the night.'

'Yes, I'll do that. Good night.'

Solveig called out as soon as she heard her son come in.

'What were those sounds?'

'Maybe the sound of the wind coming down from Helgafell.'

'Do you think we'll have another storm?'

'It's best to be prepared for anything. It could be a very strong low pressure system.'

'Ay, I can't stand these continuous lows from Labrador.'

She had barely brought the words out when the whole house began to vibrate again, the beams grinding and creaking, the cups and saucers clattering in the kitchen.

'Oh dear Jesus,' she called, 'it's an earthquake!'

They stood petrified and listened until the tremor passed and the sound of it could be heard in the distance.

'That doesn't have to be anything serious, Mama. Maybe a tremor in Hekla or Katla. For a long time the geologists have been expecting Katla to erupt. It is long overdue.'

'Let's hope so,' said his mother and heaved a sigh. 'I remember that Grandma sometimes told me about big earthquakes in the South when she was a child. Some farm houses were pushed over and people covered with rubble.'

She rubbed her hands together and tried to appear calm.

'Construction is much better now than it used to be,' he assured his mother. 'Concrete houses are now reinforced and can take a really hard jolt, and wooden houses are so pliable.'

But it wasn't the time to bring up events from the distant past: the earth shook and shuddered.

Andri went to the window and peered in the direction of the mainland, but it was pitch black, nothing visible but the glaciers. Solveig looked out another window.

'The lights are on in many of the houses around here,' she called.

At that moment a great roar went through the air overhead.

'That must have been an airplane,' she said.

'A jet,' said Andri and listened to the noise die away in the distance.

'It was as if it were just over the roof,' his mother said.

'And what's that?' she exclaimed.

'It's the light of flares, maybe from the rescue squad.'

'Or boys with rockets from New Year's Eve.'

Andri went back out onto the steps. People in the house across the street were also out on the pavement looking around.

'It must be a grass fire,' he could hear them saying to each other.

'Yes, some boys probably set the grass on fire above Kirkjubær.'

'What do you think it is?' asked Solveig when he came back into the living room. 'It's as if no one can go to bed, and I feel tense myself.'

'I'm so sleepy I can hardly keep my eyes open.'

'I have to take something relaxing,' his mother said and went back to the bathroom.

But the disturbance got worse. The house groaned and creaked and they could hear booming and rumbling. One tremor followed another.

The traffic outside sounded as if it were broad daylight, but there was much more of it.

Solveig came out of the bathroom, her face glistening with udder grease.

'I can't go to bed with all that noise and clamour outside. I don't recall an earthquake like this the year Surtsey came up.'

Andri stood in the middle of the floor and listened. He felt the blood drain from his head as his ears picked up the cry outside: Eruption! Could it be? Had Surtsey gone back again, or another new island risen from the bottom of the sea?

He ran outside. A glow of fire met his eyes over the roof of the house next door. People thronged the streets and cars couldn't get through. People called out in a great uproar, 'Helgafell's erupting, Helgafell's erupting.'

'Is it an eruption?'

'Yes, the ground is burning – it's an eruption of Helgafell.'

Men and women were running in and out of the neighbouring houses.

Andri heard his mother inside let out a terrified scream.

There was the wail of a police siren and a voice called out on a loud speaker that Helgafell was erupting and that people should get dressed in warm clothing immediately and then go directly down to the harbour, where the fishing fleet was ready and waiting.

A man from the rescue squad went into the houses along the street and told people that the Civil Defence headquarters in Reykjavik had been notified and that they had ordered all residents of the town to leave their homes immediately. There was imminent danger of the volcano's exploding at any moment and sending a stream of molten lava down over the town.

'Are our lives in danger?' Solveig whispered when the man had explained the situation.

'Yes, we can't take any chances, but we're very lucky that

the fleet is still in the harbour on account of the storm over the weekend.'

'Do we have to go in boats to the mainland?' Solveig's face trembled with emotion, and she had wiped off most of the grease.

'They are good ships,' the man said. 'They will try to take elderly and sick people to the airport if it's still useable by then.'

The man hastened back out.

'What can we take with us?' she called after him.

'Nothing but clothing. Saving lives has to take priority.'

'Mama, dress as well and warmly as you can, I'm just going to run up to see what things look like.'

Andri had put on his field jacket with the sheep-skin lining.

'Oh no, I'm so scared to be by myself,' she wailed.

'I'll just be a second. There's no danger in the meantime.'

He went over to her and tried to revive her spirits, reminding her that there had often been eruptions in Iceland without explosions or people's lives being in immediate danger, but it was the duty of the Civil Defence to make too much rather than too little out of the danger, in order to get people to obey. She could be entirely at ease while he went out for only a few minutes.

She burst into tears in her son's arms.

'I don't believe this. It's got to be a dream,' she murmured and sniffed. 'It can't be reality. . . .'

He kissed her lightly on the forehead.

'I won't be a moment,' he said. 'Dress in the warmest clothes you own.'

He rushed out and joined other people going up the street toward the volcano.

When they got up in front of the houses they saw a row of erupting craters in the black winter night, all the way from the slopes of Helgafell slanting down toward the sea. Pillars of fire rose and fell with roars and thuds, and in some places tongues of fire streamed high into the sky, which was hidden by a great cloud of ash, while glowing red rivers of quick-flowing lava rushed before their eyes in the direction of the shore, and out from this glowing lava river red and yellow branches streamed down the slopes like golden lace on a black dress.

An unearthly brown fog hung over the heaths and hay field of Kirkjubær, and the buildings were obviously defenceless against the impending danger.

Andri stared at the farm buildings in the red light of the eruption. He had been here often as a boy when he would come for a can of milk for his mother, and they had always been nice to him.

Up on the roof of the barn was a cloud of white smoke, most likely from a fire in the hay.

When he came closer he saw people were driving cows out of the cowshed. They bellowed pathetically as they emerged into the hazy red night.

A little boy stood at a distance and shouted to the people who happened to come by, 'I saw the earth split, I saw pieces of sod fly high in the air – yeah, I saw the earth open like a zipper.'

'I saw it too,' a boy of the same age said, 'I saw the fire gush up out of the ground and pieces of sod fly in every direction.'

A horse with sparks in its mane ran along the barbed-wire fence. Further along, people had pushed it down, but the horse was too frenzied to be able to get its bearings. Glowing round stones thrust high into the air and long trails of flying sparks were visible through the brownish red smoke that hung over the mountain.

Andri turned and hurried back.

His mother stood in the doorway when he came to their house, on which the red winter night was casting its perilous glow.

67

'Are the buildings at Kirkjubær in danger?' she called as she saw him.

'Yes, they'll probably catch fire tonight. They had let the cows out of the stalls and were carrying things out of the buildings.'

'Oh dear God, what will happen to us now?' she sighed.

'I think Helgafell will spare the town,' he said. 'As far as I can see the lava mainly will run the most direct way down to the sea.'

She embraced him joyfully when he walked in, and he went straight down to get the suitcases in the cellar. A policeman came up the stairs and told them the same thing the rescue squad man had said a few minutes earlier: get well prepared and then go down to the harbour where the boats would take them to Thorlaks Harbour.

'I'm so afraid I'll get seasick,' Solveig said to her son when the policeman was gone.

'Oh, no, the sea is very calm now. The good luck in the bad is that the weather isn't the same as it was on Sunday.'

'Do you think the insurance will pay for all this?' she asked him.

'We don't have time to wonder about that now.'

'I have to try to call my cousin Gústa, we'll need to stay with her when we get to Reykjavik.'

While she went to the phone and tried several times to call, Andri went upstairs to get ready for the boat trip.

She was still trying to call when he came down.

'I can't get a line.'

'No, it's no use trying to call – besides, Gústa is certainly fast asleep.'

In a little while they were ready to go. Solveig had put on slacks and a turtle-neck sweater, with a mink coat over that and a fur hat. Dressed that way she looked short and stout.

'I brought all my jewelry with me,' she said.

In the street there were trucks that took people's luggage, while others were in their own cars. They walked after the trucks down to the wharf where a large number of people had gathered. It took a long time to move forward because of the crowd and the vehicles that people had left there.

It began to drizzle, with a light easterly wind. The sky was pitch dark.

People crowded down to the pier, where the boats were taking on baggage of every description – bundles, bags, baby carriages, and whatever people had snatched up in flight. Policemen shouted to the people not to crowd too much because they could easily fall into the water between the pier and the boats. One after another the boats took on the refugees. In some places they adopted the solution of putting all the baggage into a loading net and then lifting it all at one time aboard the boat.

A little girl dressed warmly in a shawl stood right by Andri and his mother, pale in the glare of the spot lights on the freezing plant. She held a half-grown cat in her arms, and by her side her mother had a baby in a bundle. Unperceived by anyone, the cat succeeded in slipping out of the little girl's arms, who wailed loudly as soon as she realized that her cat had disappeared. Suddenly it was as if everyone around the mother and daughter had no worry more serious than the disappearance of the kitten, and the mother tried to calm her daughter who was inconsolable with grief.

At last Andri and his mother were aboard the boat, the lines were released, and the boat edged from land and another one moved up to its place at the pier.

Andri looked back at the people who were waiting to get out of the danger zone as quickly as possible. An erupting series of craters lit up the dark midwinter night. Dark brown cloud banks hung over the town, while down along the boulder-strewn beach, white puffs of steam gushed up where the glowing rivers of lava ran out into the cold sea.

Howard hadn't wakened Old Ella to let her know about the eruption. He thought there would be relatively little danger that far west in the town. But now he learned that men had been sent to people's houses to let them know about the danger and that old people and invalids would be helped to a safe place.

He saw from some distance away that the lights were on in the old woman's apartment, and it occurred to him that perhaps someone was in the process of moving her out. He knocked lightly on her door, but it was usually unlocked and he walked into the hallway. He was met by the aroma of coffee. Old Ella had heard him and opened her door into the hallway. She was fully dressed and her thin grey hair pinned up.

'It's good you came,' she said, 'I was brewing coffee.'

'I'm afraid there isn't time for coffee now,' he said, looking around to see whether she had packed a suitcase, but none was in sight.

'What kind of a hullabaloo is this really?' she asked, and put her hand on the coffee pot.

'Do you hear the booming?'

'I don't hear as well as I used to, and sometimes I'm just as glad.'

A good-natured twinkle appeared in her eyes. She went to the kitchen cabinet and took down cups and saucers.

'The Civil Defence has sent out an order to all the residents here that they have to leave their homes immediately because a serious danger threatens the town. Older people and invalids can fly over to the mainland, to a safe place.'

'Sit down,' she said and pointed to a kitchen stool. 'I have been through eruptions before.'

'No, there isn't time,' he said nervously and did not sit down. 'We ought to do as we have been told.'

She picked up a cup and saucer and poured steaming coffee into the cup.

70

'There's always time for a cup of coffee,' she said.

Howard sat on the stool, not having the heart to refuse her invitation.

'I've got some crullers here,' she said and brought out a dark tin box.

'No thanks, I don't want any.' He picked up a sugar cube.

'You should get ready, they could be here at any moment to get you.'

'Who?' she said, as if she had heard him now for the first time.

'The rescue squad from Civil Defence.'

'Oh yes, the dear men, they don't need to worry about me.'

'Those are their orders.'

He sipped from the cup. The coffee was strong and refreshing. She had sat down herself on the warming box, which had once been used to keep food warm when someone in the family wasn't at the table, but hadn't been used now for a decade and had ended up in the kitchen.

'If the electricity goes off – as could happen at any moment – then you won't be able to make coffee,' Howard said.

'Oh, I guess I could manage if the electricity goes,' the old woman said, 'we haven't always had the electricity, oh no, there was a time when it wasn't heard of in this country.'

'There could be an explosion in the mountain and a flood of lava cover the town.'

'Oh, no, there won't be any flood of lava in the town,' said the old woman, reaching for a lump of sugar in the bowl next to him.

She sat back down on the warming box. 'The Consul always wanted to have an oil stove in case it went out, and it has sometimes happened that we have used it.'

'But the lights go then too.'

'The lights, oh, no, the Consul always saw to it that we had plenty of candles, and I think there are still an awful lot of them, and also an oil lamp up in the attic, which didn't give bad light at all in its time. No one turned up their nose at it.'

'I'm still afraid that you won't be able to avoid leaving.'

'Hmm, I wonder if they will take me out forcibly,' she asked as calmly as before but with a bit more spirit.

'No, in this house no one will touch you,' Howard said emphatically.

'Because I would not have believed it of the Consul's people.'

'You put me in a very difficult position.'

'No, I may not leave. The Consul doesn't want me to go from here.'

'The Consul?'

'Yes, your uncle. He wants me to stay here in peace.'

'Have you been in touch with him?'

'How you do ask questions, son. Don't you want some more coffee?'

'Yes, maybe ten drops.'

She poured into his cup until he said to stop.

'You won't be moved forcibly,' Howard said, 'that's out of the question. . . .'

'I was a little girl here in the Islands when we had a big earthquake around the turn of the century. The bird cliffs were jostled but no lives were lost then, through God's mercy, and it will be so again.'

'Let's hope so.'

'The Consul says that nothing will happen to this house. He wants me to stay here in peace and I will do that.'

'As you wish,' said Howard and finished the cup.

'As he wishes,' the old woman corrected him.

Howard stood up.

'I will talk to Fru Camilla the first thing in the morning. I know she will want desperately to have you come to her, now Sara is home from France. I remember that Frimann told me his children thought of you as their grandmother, so it would be natural for you to go to them. But I will explain to her that you are not coming right now, and so I thank you for the coffee.'

'You're welcome,' said Old Ella and stood up. She went with him down the hallway.

'I am also staying,' said Howard, 'so you won't be alone in the house.'

'I'm never alone,' she answered in the doorway as Howard put on his hat and disappeared into the darkness.

*

Andri went with his mother down into the cabin, where the women and children had settled themselves. He succeeded in finding a seat for her and then went back up on account of the crowding below.

Solveig stayed behind in the cabin.

She recognized most of the faces around her but didn't feel like talking to anyone. The anxiety which she tried to keep under firm control had paralyzed all her loquacity. She had folded up her fur coat by her side to put her head down on. Around her she heard people whispering. There was Bubba from the bakery.

At a dance many years ago they had both danced themselves hot and flushed competing for a young first-mate with dark hair falling into his eyes and blood-red lips. He had danced with each of them in turn until the last dance was announced and Solla was blissful in the young man's arms.

The result was that Bubba escaped being a widow in the bloom of life, marrying instead her father's apprentice in the bakery, a flabby doughboy who never went to sea and never put his life in danger.

'What! Is that you Solla, dear?' Bubba called to her.

'Yes, something of me,' answered Solveig somewhat reluctantly, not in the mood to be her soul-mate.

73

'Isn't Andri with you?'

'Yes, he's probably up on the deck.'

'To think, we have to sit here like refugee women.'

'What else are we?'

'Well, that's true, but when I can't understand anything that's happening, I need to say that things will get better.'

Her daughter, light-haired and looking ill, sat beside her with a baby sleeping in her arms.

'I dreamed about this,' Bubba said after a moment's pause.

'Really?'

'Yes, one time in the autumn I dreamed that the moon shattered over the town and people rushed in every direction and down to the harbour just like it is now. Don't you remember I told you my dream, Stulla?'

Her daughter mumbled something and blinked her eyes.

'I could see it vividly when we came down to the harbour tonight, exactly like it was in the dream. . . .'

On the radio a geologist was describing the eruption with booming and thundering in the background. He said that a fifty-metre high crest of lava had built up along the full length of the eruption, with no lava flowing in the direction of the town but running instead toward the sea.

You could hear people sigh that maybe the town would escape – God grant that it escape. The geologist said that he expected the eruption to shorten at both ends and a crater to build up in the middle, resulting in great danger to the town, because the higher the crater got the greater the danger. . . .

'At first we thought that all the houses around us would burn,' Bubba continued after some moments.

The infant had waked up and began to fuss. The young mother tried to settle it back down.

'They came to us with the kids half dressed,' said Bubba and looked at her daughter.

'Are you feeling sick, dear?'

'I'm not feeling well,' the young woman groaned. On the bench lay a larger child sleeping.

'They had just moved into the new house,' Bubba said, 'that wonderful house.'

'First we drove over to my brother-in-law's, who lives on the west side of town,' said another woman, 'then we came down to the harbour. We don't have anything with us except the clothes we're wearing and one handbag, we were so afraid that the mountain would explode. Little Bjossi doesn't even have any socks.'

'I don't have much besides diapers and baby clothes in this case,' said the woman beside her, 'and my husband stayed behind. . . .'

'Helgafell must still save the town,' an old man said, breaking the silence, 'the ancient people worshipped the mountain and called it Helgafell for that reason, which was not entirely absurd, you can believe it. . . .'

'It makes a big difference that the fissure should form on its slopes and not go through it,' said his seat companion. They continued to discuss the state of the eruption.

'Steini, my son-in-law, stayed behind to try to save something from the house. Can you believe they had just acquired wall-to-wall Axminster carpet, and that can't be saved,' Bubba went on.

On the radio the geologist was tracing the history of the formation of the islands, which had been formed tens of thousands of years ago from volcanic fissures on the ocean floor that ran all the way from the Azores in the south up to the Arctic Ocean. He said that the most recent eruption of Helgafell had occurred five thousand years ago.

'It's not likely that anyone had insurance for that eruption,' said Bubba and tried to laugh.

'You're not funny, Mama,' her daughter said reproachfully.

'No, I just meant five thousand years, that was a while

back.'

'And the eruption on Surtsey,' said the man who believed in the mysterious power of Helgafell.

'Oh Surtsey is so far out in the ocean.'

'It's the same fissure,' said the man.

'If the lava closes the entrance to the harbour,' said his companion, 'then Westman Islands is finished as a fishing town.'

The boat had begun to pitch more deeply than before, and seasickness announced itself. The stench of vomit blended with the heavy cigarette smoke in the cabin. Children cried and women retched and moaned.

'Open the cabin,' someone called, 'so fresh air can get down here.'

Solveig recognized the voice of the school mistress who often came into her store to buy the Danish magazines. She was telling about her trip abroad the summer before. She had gone with Tjæreborg to Rome, and from there to Sorrento and Amalfi. Italian place names played on her lips. She had seen the ruins of Pompei, which Vesuvius had laid waste in an unexpected eruption more than two thousand years ago. The city had been buried and forgotten until a few decades ago, when it was dug up again and shown to tourists.

'Imagine,' the school mistress said near the doorway, 'such poisonous fumes accompanied the eruption that people died in the poses they were in when they breathed the fumes.'

'That is an advantage in this case,' said a man near her, 'that this eruption is a lava eruption, which people can get away from.'

'I saw casts of people in all sorts of positions,' the school mistress continued, 'even a man who was having intercourse with a goat.'

A silence came over the group after this description by the traveller.

'But we don't have any goats,' popped out of Bubba.

Her daughter scolded her, but no one seemed to have heard the unsuccessful joke.

Andri came down the stairs with raw, cold ocean air in his wake.

'Here comes Andri,' said Bubba. He nodded to her.

'Can you sit here?' his mothered whispered to him.

'Sure, I can find a place,' he said and sat down on the floor in front of her.

The boat turned and pitched on the waves while the half-sleeping people murmured. The continuous rumble of the engine was putting the passengers to sleep.

She felt her son's head rest on her knee. He is the only thing I have and live for, she thought. Much could have been different in her life if it hadn't been him whom she had to consider first and foremost. She remembered the dentist in Reykjavik who had courted her ardently, taking her horseback riding and on skiing trips to Kerlingarfjoll. But Andri had for some reason been so put off by him that she saw it would be pointless to continue the relationship.

'What do you think of Howard?' she whispered to her son.

'What about him?' he asked sleepily.

'Sigga at the office told me she had heard him talking to Frimann's widow on the telephone and that he had said he missed her and had called her 'darling.' He was pretty ridiculous here in the old days when he was chasing after birds in every direction, in his white sneakers and with his bino-culars, but now he has become such a man of the world. . . .'

And wasn't she herself really a woman of the world, even though she hadn't had the opportunity to develop those abilities in herself? She was really born to partake of life in a large city and not be cooped up in a weather-beaten fishing village. Why, hadn't the Danish chemist told her he wanted to take her with him to Århus, and it might have been fun maybe to live in

Denmark, and even to be Madame Chemist.

Or when she was first widowed and intended to move to Reykjavik and the Consul came and offered her a good job working for him – and then later when she still wanted to go and he helped her get a bookseller's licence and loaned her the money to start the store. Yes, she had often been on the verge of moving away, always dreamed of the great world awaiting her, yes ever since she first went upstairs to Frimann and he played 'On the Sunny Side of the Street' for her. . . . She had always longed to go out into the world and really get to be on the sunny side of life.

But that hadn't happened. Frimann went to America and didn't let her hear any more from him. And everyday life set in. . . .

With a young son whom she loved she retired from life, and couldn't plunge into an adventure. She sacrificed herself for him.

On the radio, an announcement was being read from the Red Cross that people shouldn't worry about what would happen to them. Places would be found for everyone, in private homes, hospitals, institutions, and other space that became available. By this time they had moved many elderly people from the old peoples' home and the hospital to the mainland with airplanes and helicopters.

On the airfield the planes waited to take off. . . .

Andri stirred.

'Were you having a dream?' his mother asked.

'Just some craziness.' He was sweating.

'It is really good that I bought government bonds,' she whispered, 'they are reliable.'

'Yes, they have increased a lot in price,' he answered in a sleepy voice.

'I owe it to Keli that I happened to buy them.'

Andri stood up.

78

'Where are you going?' asked his mother.

'The air is so heavy in here,' he said and went forward to the door.

Outside men were arguing about whether the airport had been closed.

Andri went up the stairs, where he was met by cold, raw morning air.

Men stood in heavy jackets up on the deck and watched the sailing lights of the boats in a long line in front of them, like automobile traffic in a big city at night.

Over the glaciers was the glow of daybreak, but the sea was rough and lead-grey in the twilight.

'There are the lights of Thorlaks Harbour,' said an old man with a sharp nose sticking out of his parka hood. In the dim distance might faintly be seen a few lights scattered on a black empty beach.

'That is all one harbourless stretch,' he said.

They immediately felt that the boat had changed its motion and that the swells were no longer as heavy as before.

A bit at a time the light became brighter and the boulder-strewn beach and buildings began to appear. White caps broke on skerries far out from land.

'It wasn't unreasonable for people to call on St. Thorlak to get through the skerries,' said the old man, who had slid his hood back. He had a knitted hat on his head.

In the channel where there was a gap between the skerries the sea was smoother. Spotlights were directed out at the harbour entrance and the boat slowed up considerably. Women and children came up on deck. Above the pier could be made out a fleet of busses awaiting the refugees. One after another the boats went into the channel, in behind the harbour wall and turned up to the wharf and piers.

Andri and his mother waited at the rail while the boat docked. It was low tide and a long way up to the pier. Quickly a ladder was lowered to the deck and countless hands up above steadied people and helped them up to the wet and slippery pier. Later the baggage was passed from hand to hand up out of the boat.

When all the passengers had found their luggage, places were found for them in the waiting busses.

Andri and his mother were on their way to the capital and it had still not become noticeably lighter out.

The bus began moving with a low grating sound through the sleeping town. In only a single window was there a light.

They had to drive out of town on a road riddled with potholes until they reached the main highway, up on higher ground. The people jounced together on the bad road. On the radio endless announcements were directed to the refugees, between which light music was played, as on election night. The yellow gleam of dawn slowly rose over the glaciers. The bus laboured up the winding mountain road with a deep rumbling and the people dozed in its warmth. Nothing was audible but the radio and the anaesthetizing drone of the engine. The streaks of snow on the mountain slopes were suddenly down next to the bus and accompanied it for a long way across the highlands. The progress of the bus could soon be detected in the decreased sound of the engine as it began to descend, and the snow patches departed, like a dog who gives up chasing the car and heads for home. The car lights illuminated the yellow-green moss on the lava along the roadside. Then came the fields of gravel, and soon their eyes were met with a glittering brilliance of light, long and thin over the low-lying heath.

'There are the lights of Reykjavik,' he said to his mother.

'Oh I feel awful,' she groaned, 'I hope I'm not going to have an attack.'

'There's only a little way to go.'

They drove past summer cottages waiting for spring, forsaken and deserted, and further down, a gentle river began to run along the road in graceful bends, without any hurry, between banks that were pale with last year's grass in the grey morning light.

People were beginning to talk to each other about what lay ahead for them.

'We can certainly stay with cousin Gústa,' Solveig whispered to her son.

'Don't worry about that,' he answered.

Before they knew it they were in the outskirts of the capital, with people on their way to work in comfortable morning daylight, people who had slept tranquilly through the night, oblivious to any impending danger.

They didn't stop before they had come down to the harbour, where the Civil Defence had set up a facility to receive the refugees. Andri succeeded immediately in finding a doctor to examine his mother. The doctor listened with his stethoscope, took down a quick medical history, and then decided that she should go for treatment to Vifilsstadir.

She was taken there in an ambulance. Andri stayed with her until she came into the custody of a doctor and medical staff, who offered her a warm reception.

II

After Andri had taken his mother to Vifilstadir he went back to the city.

He went to a restaurant downtown where every table seemed full, but he was able to find a place next to a man with big teeth and thick glasses.

There was a great deal of talk among the people at the next table about the effects of the eruption on the national economy.

'The first thing the government will do,' said one of them with great assurance and gravity, 'is to devalue the krona.'

'That's in the works regardless,' interjected one of his companions vigorously.

'Well, now they have something that people will have to take seriously and come to terms with. They can blame the eruption.'

Andri ordered a meat dish with curry sauce when the waitress could finally get around to take his order. He had become hungry.

When the news came on, and the announcer began to review events in Westman Islands, people stopped chattering and the dishes and silver fell silent.

A newsman described infernal fires reaching up to the sky and glowing sulphur rain, while in the background the craters could be heard in a deep voice clearing their throats. Many houses had soon fallen victim to the lava flow, but as yet there had been no loss of life and most of the five thousand inhabitants of the town had left their homes and sought refuge on the mainland in fishing boats. If the harbour was filled by lava and the town buried in volcanic ash it would be an irreparable loss for the national economy as a whole and would affect the interest of every person in the country. . . .

Then came a short interview with a geologist, who began by explaining that to him personally the eruption looked bad. It was the same kind as the Surtsey eruption a few years ago, which had gone on for three years, and for this reason one might expect the worst. The lava could be coming from a depth of ten kilometres, out of the bowels of the earth, at a temperature of about 1,100 degrees Celcius. If it should suddenly stop, then it could start up in a new fissure soon after.

After that, the president addressed the nation in great seriousness, calling upon all citizens to make an effort to assist the refugees. 'This small nation is much like a large family which knows that what happens to one happens to all,' the president said.

After lunch Andri went to the airline office and asked about flights. He was told that no one could go to the Islands without special permission from the Civil Defence, and in addition that it was uncertain whether the airport would remain open, because of fissures in the runway.

He heard that later in the day two ships should be leaving Reykjavik harbour to bring back fish and at the same time get some of the cars that had been left on the dock during the night.

Andri used the time before the ships left to go to various publishers and arrange for a postponement of his report on the year's sales. He had made good progress toward putting together the list that was due every February of books in their shop that had not been sold in the past year.

It had become dark when he came to the harbour where the ships were preparing for departure. A large crowd was in the way. People stood by the gangplank but the crew prevented anyone from coming aboard who did not have a stamped permit from Civil Defence. People were very upset because few of them had acquired such papers and they said it would be intolerable if they were hindered from going home and looking after their possessions and trying to save what they could before it was too late. It was close to becoming a free-for-all, but finally Andri succeeded in getting aboard even though he did not have the required papers. The ship was jam packed with people and it was clear that most of them would have to spend the night wherever they could find a place to lie down.

Rumours were going round that the entrance to the harbour in the Islands was closing and therefore it was unlikely that the ships could dock at the pier. Others said that the lava stream was headed down the slopes of the mountain in the direction of the town and that it was only a question of time before the glowing river of lava flooded over and submerged it all.

Andri had found a place in the smoking saloon, where people were sitting on the floor. Many of them hadn't slept during the night and were upset over the bad news that was circulating. Others said that no attention should be paid to these rumours, the harbour was in no immediate danger and the lava was still running in a quite different direction from the town.

All at once Andri was startled to see standing before him a smiling young girl in high tight leather boots, in a yellow windbreaker with a hood at the nape of her neck. She had a large quantity of black hair that fell to her shoulders.

'Don't you know me?' she asked in good spirits.

'Sara! I wasn't expecting to see you.'

'Is there any room there by you?' she asked.

'Sure, if you don't mind the floor, the rug is really thick and soft.'

She sat beside him.

'Are you going back?' she asked.

'Yes, I brought my mother this morning. But you, did you get a stamp?'

'Oh dear, I'm well stamped,' she said and took out her permit. 'I have to get Old Ella. Howard talked to Mama this morning and I was longing to go fetch her, even though it meant that I had to get away from Mama.'

She laughed, her teeth white and regular, her lips thin and long.

'I haven't seen you since you played with a jump rope on the pavement in front of your grandfather's house.'

'Yes, it's been an eternity since I've come to the Islands.'

Furtively, he contemplated her: a little bit foreign, with cream coloured skin and slightly slanting eyes.

'Haven't you just come from France?'

'Oh, no, that was months ago. Daddy came and got me – of course you heard about that?'

'No,' he lied.

'Yes, I can see you have,' she laughed, 'and it's all the same to me if half of it was a lie. But Daddy came for me in France, that's true, and everyone in the embassy flipped out, they just went crazy.'

She laughed and fun lit up her dark eyes.

'I was put in gaol as an accomplice to drug smuggling, that's also true, but I really didn't have any idea that the boys had grass and other stuff hidden in the car, I swear. My girlfriend and I were coming from Spain and we caught a ride with them just before we got to the border – which is where the customs found it. It was horrible. Of course I was immediately classified as a hopeless drug addict and all that – and poor Daddy – no, we'll skip that. . . .'

She brought out a blue pack of Gaulois and offered him one, but he declined.

She snapped a lighter and drew the flame into the cigarette.

'And what about you?' she asked, 'the last I heard of you I think you were in medical school. You're a doctor, maybe?'

'Oh no, I never will be. Poor Mama thought that I was going to be a doctor, and I let her go on believing so – while I just hung around.'

'You got to be a famous poet in school.'

She looked directly in his face, her nose was narrow and a little Indian looking.

'That is probably the surest way to go wrong.'

'What do you mean by 'go wrong'?' She drew the smoke in deeply.

'People go wrong when they believe they've been successful.'

'What is it to be successful?'

'It's just a phrase.'

'Yes you've been successful, it's easy to see it in you. You're so superior.'

'You used to be much haughtier,' he answered sharply.

'Haughty! It's just that I had a crush on you, which made me so shy whenever you spoke to me.'

'Well, is this who I think it is, this isn't Sara herself?' said the stout, closely cropped ship's captain who had come waddling toward them.

'Yes, a bit of me,' she said and rose to her feet.

'What are you doing going to the Islands now?'

'I'm just going to get Old Ella, she doesn't want to leave.'

'No, the old lady won't go as long as the Consul's house is left standing.'

'Mama is determined that she move in with us.'

'Come and greet some old friends of your father's,' he said and took her arm and led her to a table where some ship owners sat together discussing the current situation and what lay ahead.

'We've finished taking women and children to the mainland,' he said, 'and the next thing is to save the fishing equipment. We won't have fishing equipment for the fleet this season if it is lost now, because the time required to order it from Japan is so long.'

'Isn't there any other country than Japan?'

'No, they are the only people who know how to make the

86

kind of nets we need. . . .'

His companions greeted Sara when they understood who she was and invited her to sit with them. They began to recall the good old days when the Consul was like a king on the chessboard and they themselves were just pawns.

'Wasn't he something of a tyrant?'

They laughed at her question.

'Oh yes, he could be damned hard, your grandfather.'

'He was sometimes caricatured in *The Mirror* as a hedgehog,' one of them said.

Andri sat by himself and began to go over in his mind what he had heard about Sara. She had certainly moved into a bad crowd in Paris – she was seen in the company of Arabs and all kinds of riffraff – her parents had been seriously worried about her – she was their only child after her brother Rikki died. Andri remembered her as a little girl in bobby socks outside the Consul's house when her family lived there before the accident, but she had barely been seen in the Islands since.

*

'There is so much that I need to ask you about,' said Sara as she sat back down beside him. 'You were recalling the pavement outside my grandfather's house, and I remember it so well, with all the dandelions.'

'Now it's all cracked and disintegrating.'

'Yes, the world has disintegrated considerably since then.'

'That's true, it has.'

'I remember that grandpa always wore a high collar.'

'Yes, he was in the old style.'

'I don't think he was very well liked.'

'He was liked by the people who worked for him. Mama, for example, thought the world of him. She worked for him in the office first.'

'Oh yes, your mother.' Sara laughed. 'I can believe she thought a lot of him. Didn't people say that she had an affair with him?'

Andri was taken aback by such a point-blank question.

'Please don't pull into your shell because I ask so directly. It wouldn't make any difference to me if Mama had an affair with someone. In fact, I would rather she did because then she would not be quite so insufferable.'

'Yes, I've heard that Mama had an affair with him, but I. . . .'

'It wasn't so foolish of her, she was really very sexy.'

'Yes, I suppose so.'

'She was getting fat the last time I saw her.'

'Yes, she likes chocolate.'

'Didn't she have red hair?'

'Yes, once. Your grandfather did a lot for her when she became a widow. Seamen weren't insured then as they are now.'

'I wish there was someone who wanted to have an affair with Mama. She is trying to completely destroy me since I came home.'

'Really?'

'She blames me for Daddy's dying of a heart attack.'

'How can she do that?'

'Because it was such a blow to him when I got in trouble, and he had to get me out of prison.'

'Is it really true that you went to prison?'

'It began with Mama and Daddy being determined to put me into an English school. I didn't see a man there from one week to the next, except the monk who came sometimes on his bicycle with potatoes. I was going completely insane – and so of course I ended up getting gonorrhoea.'

'I certainly haven't been as famous as catching gonorrhoea,' said Andri, without allowing himself to appear shocked.

'Really?'

'I'm so immature.'

'I didn't realize it right away. Naturally I was expelled from school, which was really a blessing from heaven because England is such a dump. O.K., let's talk about something else, but so that you don't misunderstand me I don't want you to think I am any better than I am.'

'You don't have to worry about that here, but I am sure that you are better by half than you think you are.'

'Oh no, that's why the old guy wanted to show me off before, not at all because of Daddy who they don't give a damn about now that he's dead, or grandpa who domineered over everyone who came near him and crushed grandma's spirit so she died in a clinic in Denmark – oh no, it was just because I am notorious and have been in a French prison, where everything is crawling with lice and the toilet is a hole in the floor.'

She took a cigarette from the blue pack with a quick movement of her hand.

'You knew my brother Rikki, didn't you?'

'Yes we and Kalli played together sometimes.'

'Yes, Kalli. He was with Rikki when he fell. Old Ella told me that.'

'They were netting puffins. It had rained and the grass was slippery.'

'That wasn't why he fell.'

'Really? Why was it?'

'They were wrestling over a knife that Rikki owned.'

'I remember that knife. It was Swiss, red with a white cross and with many blades, even a pair of scissors. Kalli told me they had swapped knives the day before Rikki fell.'

'He cheated Rikki, they swapped the knives sight unseen – and Kalli didn't own anything but an ordinary fish knife.'

'How do you know they were wrestling?'

'That's what I was told.'

'There were only the two of them.'

'I saw it in a dream.'

'A dream?'

'Yes, I sometimes dream some unusual dreams. I sometimes dream about Daddy.'

'What is he like?'

'He is lying on the kitchen floor in front of the refrigerator, just like we found him in the morning, and the milk is boiling up all over everything, and I run to him and want to raise him to his feet, but he is paralyzed and when I lift up his head his tongue hangs out of one side of his mouth—it is so horrible that I wake up screaming to myself.'

The news broadcast on the radio had been turned up in the smoking saloon so that all the passengers could hear it, forward in the passageways and anywhere else that people had found a place to lie down.

The commentator said the eruption was eight hundred metres long in several sections, and the fissure in the earth's surface reached far out into the sea. The lava was mostly chunks, but with an increasing east wind there was a danger that ash and glowing bits of lava could be carried in over the town and cause fires.

When the news of other events in the world was over, the cease-fire in Vietnam and the funeral of President Johnson, the radio was turned down again, and people began to go to bed.

*

At dawn following the night sail from Reykjavik they began to approach the glow over the dark islands, which assumed more and more of a fixed appearance: the mountain ridge with fire-spewing craters and a lava flow in countless branches down the slopes and out into the sea, where gushed up huge white pillows of steam.

The harbour was still open and did not seem to be in im-mediate danger from the lava flow, but when the ship docked at the pier the columns of fire seemed menacingly close to the roofs of the houses.

A solitary hill had begun to take shape on a ridge of Helgafell where a hay field and pasture land had been before.

When Andri went ashore, new fire engines were being unloaded, which a professor of geology wanted to be used for pumping water on the glowing lava, and thus try to affect the direction of the lava stream.

Andri hurried to his house. He had left the house unlocked, in case in his absence the lava stream had headed down the slope of the mountain in the direction of the town and harbour; but it was clear that the main lava stream ran as it had from the beginning, in the most direct route to the shore.

The ash dust in the streets had increased a fair amount in the approximately twenty-four hours that had passed, and some of the houses with roofs that did not slant much had accumulated mountain-shaped piles of ashes.

There in the faint grey light of morning stood his mother's house as if it were firmly fixed in powdered ash. What had been on the steep roof, however, had mostly slid off and collected here and there in black snowdrifts.

Andri walked around the house to examine whether anything had happened to it during his absence. All the panes were unbroken in the windows. The glow of the fire gleamed in those that faced the eruption. All the gutters were full of volcanic ash which had piled up and would continue to pile up if it weren't swept down.

He went up the steps and took his shoes off in the vestibule so as not to track in on the living room floor. He felt very much deprived of sleep. Rumbling and booming came from the volcano above, but that could not keep him awake after he had thrown himself down to sleep on the living room couch.

He woke up again with a loud noise outside the window next to him, and when he looked out he saw that men in white helmets and orange coats were going with a bulldozer up toward the site of the eruption. It was now bright daylight. He went out onto the steps and called to them. They told him that work was going on to shove up a pumice wall to protect the houses against the pressure of the lava that constantly crept outward in the direction of the harbour. Several houses had been covered by the spreading of the lava.

Andri went back in and began looking for something to eat in the kitchen. Then he shaved in the bathroom, and soon he stopped being particularly aware of the booming and thundering up above. He had just finished shaving when Kalli suddenly popped through the front door in a pink coat and yellow helmet on his head. He told Andri that he had had a run-in with Howard, who had discovered a bunch of them breaking into a gasoline storage tank to get fuel for cars and boats.

'I was distributing helmets and rubber boots from a shop that was collapsing under the weight of pumice. The Jew merchant went totally out of his mind and called Howard for help.'

'And what did Howard do?'

'I told him that Jews like that ought to be exterminated like pests, and offered him a biscuit from a tin I had salvaged.'

'Didn't Howard say anything at all?'

'Oh sure, he began to babble that the man wasn't a big capitalist. By the way, I signed you up as a member of my salvage team,' said Kalli and took off his helmet.

'First I have to salvage myself before I salvage other people,' answered Andri. He offered Kalli some hot coffee that he had in the pot.

Kalli saw that he had tracked in on the floor and took off his boots.

'Corrugated iron should be nailed over all the windows that face the fire,' he said and went in stocking feet onto the kitchen floor. 'Some houses have burned when glowing pieces of lava broke window panes and set fire to curtains and rugs.'

'Is there enough corrugated iron?'

'No, there's a shortage, but a new shipment is on the way. I have enough sheets to put in front of the windows here. It could happen that your house comes into direct line of the fire before long.'

'I realize that,' answered Andri, 'and was thinking for that reason of moving down to the store.'

'There's enough room at the hotel, and it doesn't cost anything,' said Kalli.

'No, I'd rather move down to the store. A person could manage very well there, and it wouldn't come into danger before. . . .'

He hesitated to finish the sentence.

'Naturally it could happen that it too would be threatened,' he added, 'but that would be a short distance from the harbour.'

'There is a severe shortage of people to do salvage work,' said Kalli, 'and especially nailing in front of windows, but a telephone call went into Reykjavik for carpenters and about seventy have signed up.'

Andri put on some laced rubber boots that he owned and an orange coat, a helmet and work gloves that he got at a camp in vocational school. Thus equipped, he went with Kalli and some friends to nail sheets of iron over windows in the houses closest to the eruption.

Down at the harbour, ships were constantly being loaded. Cars which had been left behind on the pier were to be shipped when they finished loading frozen fish fillets and dried fish.

Andri met Howard later in the day, who told him that now the eruption was coming from fewer craters than before.

'But that doesn't necessarily mean anything except that the volcanic activity has been compressed into the middle of the fissure,' he said.

He took Andri into the packing room of the freezing plant where ordinarily a hundred women worked at this time of year, and now it was empty, except where some men were finding a place for home appliances and equipment that had been salvaged from the east side of town.

'It will be harder to get the housewives to come back,' said Howard, 'when all the furniture has been moved out of the houses and they stand empty. There was too much of a hurry. Westman Islanders have been in tight spots before, and looked each other uncertainly in the eye without turning pale.'

'Will the boats take their catches to the mainland?' asked Andri.

'Yes, it is hopeless to land them here as things stand,' Howard answered, 'although we could take capelin. We have a capelin tank with a superstructure, and capelin processing requires only a few people.'

Andri wanted to ask him about Sara, but he kept quiet about that and said, 'Has anything been decided about Old Ella?'

'No, not for the moment, but she won't be taken from here against her will.'

*

Andri and Kalli were with some men who were trying to salvage the monument of Jon the Martyr, which had ended up in the lava and stood half-way out of the glowing surface.

'Did you notice before,' said Kalli, 'that there were a bunch of Americans shovelling pumice off the roof of Isborg?'

'Yes, a lot of concrete buildings have collapsed under the weight, and Howard didn't have a choice of people to do it.'

'Let them go if they can't be saved in any other way.'

'It's a simple matter for you to say that.'

'It ought to be just as simple for you to be on guard against a secret agent like Howard.'

They stood at a distance and watched as men put a cable around the stone, despite the intense heat coming from the edge of the lava.

94

'Doesn't it strike you as suspicious that a man like Howard could be content being here?' Kalli continued.

'He could have his personal reasons.'

'Like what?'

'How should I know?'

'There's bound to be something behind his being hired.'

'Why don't you ask him yourself?' said Andri.

The men lifted the stone with crowbars up onto a platform.

'I did,' answered Kalli.

'And what did he say?'

'He evaded every question.'

A school teacher had found his way up on the car beside the gravestone of Jon the Martyr and had begun to tell the incident of Reverend Jon's having been killed by pirates from Algeria.

*

In the evening when they went into the cafeteria Sara stood there by a big coffee urn and was brewing coffee. She waved to Andri who went straight to her.

'How's it going?' she asked.

'We don't have anything under control. The lava keeps inching forward, and the pumice on the roofs bursts the walls of the houses.'

'Is your house in danger?'

'It could get to be.'

'Shouldn't I come and help you move things out?'

'Yes, if you'd like to.'

'Howard would certainly lend us a truck to move your stuff.'

And so it was. The next day all three of them worked to move out of the house and put everything on a truck they had taken over from Howard. Otherwise cars were taken without permission wherever they happened to be, and it was possible to use them to move with.

'Did you hear that the Defence Force offered to find a place for the refugees in military housing on the Base?' said Kalli.

'Aren't they very nice buildings?' asked Sara.

'It's a scandal that they're moving out of practically all of the housing they used to rent from Icelanders off the Base,' Kalli said.

'Didn't they have to pay a lot higher rent than Icelanders?' asked Sara.

'That doesn't make any difference.'

'I suppose it does to the ones who are renting.'

Kalli was on the point of answering her.

'Ugh, Kalli my friend, cut the clichés about the Americans, I'm sick and tired of listening to them,' she said sharply. She was piling up phonograph records.

'Wasn't there a lot of protest in France against the Vietnam war?' Kalli asked.

'Oh sure, there were plenty of people as stupid as you.'

'I heard that you weren't in very good company in Paris.'

'I don't give a shit what you heard about me. I've never paid any attention to anything I heard about you.' She held a big stack of records in her arms.

'I'm going to have the phonograph and records with me in the store,' Andri said to her.

'We can drop them off on the way,' she answered and took the records out.

'What are you doing with this mixed-up kid?' asked Kalli when she had gone out to the truck.

'She's probably no more mixed up than we are.'

Andri picked up the sofa with Kalli and they carried it out. That made a full load on the truck. They drove away. Kalli was on the load in back, and Andri sat inside with Sara, who drove.

'I know Kalli's type,' she said, 'they are the same everywhere.'

'He's an activist and knows every cellar and barge in Amsterdam.'

'What's he doing here?'

'Waiting for the naval war with Britain.'

'On land,' laughed Sara sarcastically, 'it's just like him.'

*

They dropped in at the elementary school, but all the rooms were packed with furniture and the gymnasium was piled up to the ceiling, so they drove down to the processing room at Isborg. People were there with horses that were going to be carried over to the mainland by helicopters from the Defence Force. They would be fed by farmers of the southern lowlands for the time being.

Julius helped them unload the truck and find a place for the furniture and other stuff. He said he thought the eruption was weakening and that maybe the winter fishing season wouldn't be completely down the drain. He took back the truck when they had finished cleaning out the trash.

Andri went with Sara back to the Consul's house.

'Have you had anything decent to eat today?' she asked.

'Buttered bread in the cafeteria, which you probably buttered.'

'You should come with me and get some smoked lamb from Old Ella. She is always cooking smoked lamb for Howard and me, and I've had horrible nightmares from it.'

The smell of cooking greeted them when she opened the door to the cellar.

'I invited Andri to have smoked lamb with us,' she called into the kitchen where Old Ella sat at the centre of her domain, like a spider.

They took their boots off out in the hallway. Sara's were made of soft black leather.

Old Ella had hot coffee in the pot and Andri thought her look was almost friendly, but he avoided looking her in the eye.

The old woman sat on the warming box and Sara got her to

tell them old stories that were circulating again on account of the eruption. She said that people had only themselves to blame for things that they had been warned about, and they should have noticed the warnings.

'What shouldn't have been done?' asked Sara.

'Well, let's see,' said the old woman and began to rock back and forth.

'Tell us, we're in such suspense.'

'I don't like chattering about things like that.'

'But you will for me, won't you,' Sara pleaded.

'I expect that most people here at home remember the cistern that the brother and sister drowned in a few years ago,' she said after some reflection.

'I remember it,' said Andri. 'It was filled in with gravel.'

'That was exactly it,' the old woman grumbled.

'It shouldn't have been?' asked Sara.

'They had been warned about it,' she murmured.

'And what was a second thing?' asked Sara, not allowing the old woman's reluctance to interfere.

'There was the big stone up on the slope.'

'Do you mean where the new apartment development is going up?' asked Andri.

She nodded her head.

'Elves lived in it, and the contractor himself said that a woman in a blue cloak came to him in a dream and told him not to tamper with the stone because it was their village and her son was sick.'

'And he did it anyway?'

'He intended to stop building on the site, but they had already blown up the stone with dynamite before he knew about it. The contractor died of cancer in the autumn.'

'Wouldn't the elves have died in the blast?' asked Sara.

The old woman began to hum to herself, the pot was simmering, and the kitchen windows had steamed up.

'What was the third?' asked Sara, 'you've got us in such suspense.'

The old woman got up from the warming box and turned the burner down under the pot.

'The third, yes there's always a third – it'll only take a drop to fill the measure.'

'What was it?'

'I don't want to blame anyone,' answered the old woman, 'but the bishop's son was installed in the church this autumn.'

'And that shouldn't have happened?'

'People believed that if these three events occurred – if anything was built west of High Stone, if Cistern went dry or was filled up, and if the son of a bishop became a priest of the Islanders – then the Islands would again be pillaged by the Turks, and now all this has happened, and not by coincidence,' said the old woman sighing deeply.

They heard the hall door open upstairs and someone come in.

'Howard has come,' said Sara, 'let's go up.'

It was getting dark and Howard had lit the lamps in the living room and back in the office.

His face brightened to see them. Sara told how things were with Andri.

'May I offer you something before dinner?' he asked.

'Yes, please. I want a dry martini,' said Sara. 'What do you want, Andri?'

He thought about it.

'I usually have bourbon in America, but here I have Scotch. What do you say to that?'

'No, I think I would like a dry martini like Sara.'

'Fine.'

Howard went to the wine cabinet, which stood on three carved feet and had little windows in lead frames.

He mixed the drinks and they sat down and relaxed.

'I'm hoping that the eruption is letting up, but we don't dare allow the transport ships inside the harbour at night,' Howard said as he handed them their drinks.

He sat down and they lifted their glasses.

Suddenly it was as if nothing were going on – as if the column of fire they could see through the window, illuminating the pumice that covered the house roofs, was nothing but an evening fireworks display at a holiday amusement park.

'There's only one fire column now,' Andri said.

'But you can see that it's much broader and sturdier than the others were,' said Howard. 'Maybe all the strength of the others is concentrated in this one. The temperature of the harbour has lowered somewhat.'

'Isn't that a good sign?' asked Andri.

'I hope so.'

Howard began to tell them about a seal that had come into the harbour in front of the freezing plant. They had thrown fish to him until a few days before the eruption, when he stopped putting in his usual appearance and had not been seen since.

'He felt the changes in the sea,' said Andri.

'We've lost all sensitivity to our environment,' said Howard. 'City dwellers are not participants in any natural environment, and will therefore probably become extinct.'

'Then we can just go out into space,' said Sara, 'where we came from.'

'There's a light on a ship outside the harbour,' said Andri.

'Yes, it's a cable ship awaiting developments, in case the overseas telephone that lies on the ocean floor there should go out,' Howard said.

'What connection would we have then with other countries?' Andri asked.

'With Europe, nothing but radio.'

They heard that Old Ella had come up and was setting the table in the dining room.

'I talked to your mother today,' Howard said to Sara.

'Ugh, I'm so tired of her.'

'I told her not to worry about you . . . .'

Sara burst out laughing.

'I told her that Ella still couldn't be made to leave and that that was that. You would come with or without her when it suited you.'

Howard went to the window and pointed the telescope toward the harbour.

Steaming smoked lamb awaited them on a platter when they went into the dining room. They had scarcely finished dinner when the telephone rang. Howard went into the office. They heard it was Julius that he was talking to.

Howard came into the dining room and told them that the volcano had increased, and molten lava had broken through into a new channel.

He went to the window and turned the telescope in the direction of the volcano.

'Julius said that two houses were on fire and more were in danger.'

'We should probably go and help,' said Andri.

They went to get ready.

The wind blew straight at them when they went out.

'It's coming in the worst direction for us,' said Howard. 'Now it can set many houses on fire.'

A crowd of people was engaged in salvage work when they got there, but many houses burned that night or ended under the molten lava. Darkness, steam and falling ash swirled about the glow of the burning houses, and flying sparks were carried a long way over the coal-black town on the east wind.

*

Andri saw that it wouldn't be long before their house was in serious danger.

He and Sara went there during the night and moved various

small things down to the shop.

They sat at the kitchen table and drank coffee.

Ash, pumice and rain pounded on the house, but over everything could be heard the thunder of the volcano.

Sara had stretched her left arm out on the table, and he noticed a large scar on the inside of her forearm.

'Where did that come from?' he asked and traced along the scar with his finger tip.

'I cut my wrist.'

'What happened?'

'I couldn't see any other way.'

'Was that in prison?'

'No, it's a simple matter to be in prison. Then you only think about getting out, but when you're stuck inside yourself, and the veins are the net that holds you in, then what do you do?'

'No one can escape from himself.'

'Sometimes I lay and thought about the shore here, the rocks with all the kelp that appears when the tide goes out – and then it comes back in.'

'Did you think about the beach here at home when you were in France?'

'I saw myself lying in the sand and the waves talking to me, all nine of my sisters, what are their names again? Unnur, Alda, Bara . . . and they caressed me and wanted to take me with them into the depths where they all merge back together.'

She pulled back her hand and smiled.

'It was wonderful tonight,' she said, 'I think I have never been so free.'

'That kind of salvage work unites everyone and awakens the best in a person,' Andri agreed.

'And it gives you a sense of purpose . . . .'

She looked at the couch. 'May I lie down there? I am completely exhausted.'

'Certainly. I have bedclothes underneath it.'

'No, no bedclothes. I want to lie down in my clothes – and you can lie down with me if you promise not to fool around. I don't feel up to anything like that now.'

'Whatever you want.' He began to take books and papers off the couch so they could lie down.

She took off the sweater she had worn under her windbreaker, and was bare above the waist, except for her brassiere. Her dark hair fell around her slender shoulders. She was like a child.

'You have bronze-coloured skin,' he said.

'Probably the legacy of some Indian whom other ancestors of mine have flogged.' She slid out of her jeans. He brought a red checkered Gefjun blanket.

She was like a long-legged wading bird when she went to the couch and lay down.

He spread the blanket over her.

'Have you heard,' she said and began to snuggle under the blanket, 'that my grandfather's boats never had as good catches after my brother Rikki was killed?'

'No, who told you that?'

'On a Greek island girls were sacrificed in olden times,' she continued, 'so the harvest would be good. They were sacrificed in a special festive ceremony where they were led under a black bull. . . .'

'Don't think about that now,' he said in the darkness while he was taking off some of his clothes. Then he lay down beside her and spread some of the blanket over himself and tried to sleep with her back along his side, and he thought of the shore where her sisters call to her and try through enchantment to draw her to them in the deep.

*

Andri didn't see Sara again until several days later at a prayer service in the church. It was a small nineteenth-century

103

timber church covered with corrugated iron and half submerged in black lava sand.

He entered after the service had begun.

The priest in the pulpit recalled Jon the Martyr who was killed at the hands of the murder-crazed Algerian pirates called 'Turks' in those days. Jon had earlier admonished his flock to improve their way of life and to take the warning of God's imminent judgment to be found in earthquakes, monsters from the sea, wonders and signs in the heavens, and serious accidents.

The effort to get the Martyr's memorial out of the lava had succeeded, and people could be reminded that the Islands were quickly rebuilt after the Turkish plundering and that a prosperous life had flourished in the three hundred and fifty years that had passed since then.

And further, the priest recalled another man of God who had not lost courage though his whole neighbourhood had been surrounded by fire and a rushing lava flow. The Reverend Jon Steingrimsson had said that the fire was sent to burn the weeds out of the Lord's field and to hush the useless and petty land quarrels of the parishioners, constantly rising interest rates and a ridiculous lust for real estate. In this way God was turning people's minds away from things that could burn into little particles and was showing those who took pride in their great property what it was really worth. Is it possible, the priest continued in a whining voice, for people here and now to draw a lesson from this, or are the admonitions of that respected preacher without the meaning for us in the twentieth century that they had then? The priest fell silent and gazed like a shepherd over his flock. Every seat was filled and people stood in the back by the doors, grave and weary, everyone in work clothes, grimy faced, unshaved. Heavy rumblings came from outside.

Then the priest described how the lava threatened the church at Klaustur, where Reverend Jon Steingrimsson was with his parishioners almost two hundred years ago.

104

The church had been full of smoke and sulphur fumes, but Reverend Jon had the doors closed so the congregation could be earnest in its invocation of the Lord and its fervent prayers for mercy. And it happened when the doors were opened again that the people saw where the lava flow had stopped only a stone's throw from the church doors, and piled up there, where it may be seen to this day.

This is the clearest example that faith in the Lord can be more powerful than fear and can perform deeds of omnipotence.

And still he urged the congregation to keep that example firmly in mind and to forget not their Creator in excessive worship of appliances and comforts of life . . . .

Some of the congregation started to clear their throats and blow their noses so that the priest's weak prayer sounded a bit pathetic.

And when they came out at the end of the prayer service, the eruption was just as powerful as before and no deeds of omnipotence had been performed.

Pumice chunks clicked against the corrugated iron that had been nailed over windows, even on God's house itself. A pink light cast its strange glow in the vicinity of the fire pillar, beyond which was the night's darkness and black heaps of pumice.

'That can be an awful windbag preacher,' said Sara as she took Andri's arm on the way out of the church. 'Doesn't he know that human sacrifice is the only thing that can stop a volcano?'

'You don't think it would be enough to sacrifice cats?' answered Andri, thinking about the cats that the police had been shooting throughout the town. They were pets which had been left behind and were hungry, but all the mice and rats were said to have died of poisonous gas that had turned out to be noticeable in the cellars of houses.

'No, nothing less than human sacrifice will do,' she said,

'preferably a young girl.'

Andri was startled by her words. Was she serious? There was no other way to take it. And what could she be hinting at?

They saw houses from a distance in bright flames, the lava face constantly moving forward with a creaky rumbling, meeting no effective resistance. Everywhere people were carrying furniture and other moveable things out of the houses, rugs, even doors.

They were told that American explosives experts were going around with Icelandic geologists investigating whether it would be possible to blast a channel out of the main crater so that the lava flow could run in the other direction from the town and reduce the pressure in the direction of the harbour down at the base of the slope. People were pessimistic about the outlook. The new undersea water pipeline from the mainland had collapsed beneath the weight of the lava and they now had to use the old pipe with the expectation that the same thing would happen to it. Sea water was pumped from the harbour with diesel engines, but the hoses were entirely too small to produce any significant cooling.

Andri saw that their house was in real danger, but everything that mattered had been taken out of it. Still there were several little things which they collected now and took down to the shop.

Night had come on. Andri brewed some coffee and they sat on the couch, conscious of their friendship for each other. She told him that they should go to her house: there was a cubbyhole in the cellar she had fixed up for them.

On the way they saw that Old Ella's light was on, so they went through the inside hallway without making their presence known.

There were two storage rooms full of old things from the Consul's household, and a third which Sara had brightened up for them. Checkered curtains were at the window, a large mattress with a brown cover in the corner, a broken mirror in a gilt frame, a table that had something wrong with it and an old light-blue trunk full of party clothes from times of departed splendour.

Sara showed him a faded ball gown of her grandmother's. There was a three-corned Consul's hat, white silk scarves that had turned yellow, a corset belonging to the Consul's wife, silk stockings, patent leather shoes and other cast-off dress clothes.

Up next to the wall stood an old rocking chair with broken springs and frayed red plush upholstery.

'Rikki and I often rocked in this chair. We were so little we thought we were on a ship out at sea.'

On a stool by the mattress she had set an ornamental copper tray and arranged candle stubs on it in a ring around the edge.

'That is a tray from an Indian table. Now we can use it under the candles.'

She lighted them with a match.

'Turn off the ceiling light,' she told him, 'and lock the door.'

In the candle light their shadows flickered on the white-washed wall.

'Sometimes I think I am nothing more than a shadow of another person who is some place else in another plane,' she said and lay down on the mattress.

He bent down to her.

They heard the rumble in the volcano like surf in the distance, and all at once he felt a great desire for her.

'Undress me,' she whispered.

*

Had he slept or lain half waking?

An old incident came back to him.

He was at his friend's house in Reykjavik. The friend and his wife were at the movies. They had told him to wait there until they came back—he could play records or read a book. Their older daughter was practising the clarinet in her room. The younger one ran into the room in her bathrobe, just out of the bath tub and smelling of soap. She brought him a picture book and asked him to look at it with her. His friend had told him to have a drink of whisky – there was a drop left in the decanter – while they were away. That was fine, his nerves were still on edge after a little party the night before. The little girl fell asleep in his arms. He carried her into her bed. Then the older one began showing him her musical instrument. What happened next? He could not remember exactly, but they had got into a pillow fight. In high spirits she had thrown a pillow at him. They were making a racket, and the next thing the little sister was spying on them. The big sister started yelling at her, and the little sister started to cry – and at that moment the mother and father came home from the movies.

What was it? What exactly was going on? Tears, accusations.

The mother spoke with her daughters in turn. The big sister had locked herself in her room.

The host offered him another drink.

'How was the picture?' he asked his friend.

'It was Tati.'

'How was Tati?'

'Tati is always Tati.'

The mother storms into the room, fire in her eyes.

'I don't ever want this man to come into our home again.'

'This man.' He had become 'this man,' indicted, expelled.

She flounces back out of the room, the husband, the friend after her.

The guest empties his glass. He hears their loud talk in the back. It makes the whisky taste like green soap to him.

The father of the house comes back gravely.

'What did you do to her?'

'I didn't do anything to her, we got in a pillow fight.'

'A pillow fight?'

'Yes, I went into her room, she threw her pillow at me, I threw it back at her – and so on several times.'

'Show him the door, Jonas, I don't want to see him here any longer.'

Shouts, exclamations, door slamming.

They go toward the door. The mother has locked herself in with her daughters for protection against this horrible man . . . .

'What were you dreaming?' Sara asks when he opens his eyes.

'Just something crazy.'

'No, dreams aren't crazy, they can tell us a lot.'

Most of the candle stubs were burned out. He got dressed in the dark.

'Yes, it's best that you go now,' she said.

She went with him down the hallway scantily clad.

It was still dark out and a cold wind blew in his face as he turned away.

*

In the strong east wind about a hundred houses were buried under pumice and ash. Others fed the fire and were crushed under the lava face, which steadily crept forward.

Still, people didn't lose heart, and better organization was brought to the salvage work and to all the services. The plan of trying to blast a new channel for the lava was abandoned. The island was so sensitive to vibrations that explosions of that sort could collapse even sound houses, in addition to which the wall of lava was too thick for the blasting to give favourable results.

In some of the Reykjavik newspapers, which at times didn't appear in the Islands until they were several days old, the complaint could be seen that the Defence Force had not been thanked sufficiently for its part in the salvage work and now most recently for lending water guns, which, however, were of no greater effectiveness than anything else against the progress

109

of the lava.

Kalli scoffed at these articles over coffee in the cafeteria, saying nothing was more likely than that the NATO-ites wanted the foreign minister called home immediately from the meeting of the United Nations in order to deliver an expression of gratitude to the Defence Force for moving the Islanders' sheep and hens to the mainland.

Rebuttals of these articles had appeared, and one of the capital's afternoon papers gave much attention to a resolution that had been passed at a meeting of school students, expressing satisfaction with the eruption, because it would be a benefit to Iceland if wealthy people experienced serious losses.

Kalli read the resolution aloud to his coffee companions.

'That's nothing but the childishness in every young person, but it doesn't last for long,' said one of the men at the table after Kalli laid down the paper with a cocky smile.

'No, they're right,' Kalli responded, 'I agree completely.'

'That's why you're doing salvage work?'

'No, it doesn't follow, but Westman Islanders, who were great seamen and heroes before, have now become nothing but bourgeois who measure everything by home appliances, furniture and concrete apartment buildings, so they deserve to be reminded how little those things are worth.'

People interrupted him and told him to shut up, and stood up from the table. But Kalli was very amused.

'It is a false world that you believe in, and it will collapse. We will rebuild on its ruins,' Kalli shouted. But the men went on sipping their coffee without paying any attention to his words.

Kalli raised his voice still louder, 'and least of all should we feel any indebtedness to America. It would be better if everything was covered with ashes.'

Again there was a pause in the movement of the lava and the word went around that the temperature in the harbour had gone down several degrees.

People became hopeful again. Maybe the eruption was ending.

There was a breeze from the north, a gentle frost and clear weather. The mountain scenery, with Hekla and Öræfajökull, was distinctly visible in its winter dress, translucent white, with a blue mid-winter sky and a black foundation of pumice.

Smoke from the tall chimney of the capelin-rendering plant rose into the air, and people inhaled the pungent odour that they had often cursed before as if now it were a heart-strengthening spice. It reminded them of the time when the wheels of industrial life ground out gold day and night.

Down by the harbour Howard stood talking with Julius.

'Everything is in full swing now,' he said smiling.

'Yes, as long as the weather is like this and the ash-fall doesn't bother us.'

Julius looked in the direction of the cloud of smoke over the erupting volcano.

'The worst thing is that we don't have more trucks to move the capelin into the storage tank,' said Howard.

'They needed them to carry the pumice away.'

The tephra was hauled to the western part of the island where it would be used in the foundation under a new apartment development that had been started before the eruption began.

'I heard that a foreign company is interested in using the pumice as a building material,' Howard said.

'It's certainly possible to use it that way,' answered Julius, 'but some of the cost factors have to be worked out, such as the shipping for example.'

But the pause did not last long. The rumbling in the volcano began to increase again and such powerful explosions resounded that houses trembled and shook. Many people were afraid that the eruption would begin to spread out, but the geologists maintained that the explosions could be a good sign and might be accompanied by a reduction of the lava flow. People were soon aware that more poisonous gas was evident in the cellars of houses and in low-lying places.

It was in this sudden reversal that Sara and Andri watched his mother's house get caught in an eddy of lava, turn around in it, break apart and burn.

The last thing that Andri snatched out of it was the Rafna stove, which had served his mother well and which many Sunday roasts had been cooked in.

He put it in storage with Howard.

When he phoned his mother at Vifilsstadir the line was always busy, and when finally he did get through late at night she was not in her room and could not be located. Andri hoped that meant she was going out for a good time in the capital.

*

Howard studied a map of the Isthmus, which there was a plan to cut through if the entrance to the harbour was closed. The lava tip which had moved slowly down over the southern wall of the harbour was now only about two hundred metres from the light on the outer harbour wall.

The idea was to dig a ditch through the Isthmus north of the harbour. The channel should be about 45 metres wide and five to six metres deep, measured against the spring low tide. It would be relatively easy to do because the Isthmus was for the most part clay deposits, sand, and gravel.

On the other hand it wasn't enough to make this channel. It was also necessary to build a protective wall beyond it to protect the mouth of the entrance from surf and currents beyond the outer harbour.

Another alternative that had been discussed, if Westman Islands harbour was closed, was constructing a harbour on the mainland near Dyrhola Island. But that would be very costly.

Then Howard had plans in preparation to move everything out of the freezing plant if the harbour was closed. There were heavy, bulky sets of machines, such as huge quick-freezing chests, steam kettles, filleting machines, boilers and presses, some of which weighed many tons, to countless drying racks fastened to the walls and difficult to get loose.

In the midst of the great uncertainty that beset them, it happened that some foreign fashion models stepped unexpectedly out of an airplane near the eruption and the pumice showers. A film crew was with them, the appropriate equipment dangling from them, to film the spring fashions in a different and exciting setting.

They set up in a half buried cemetery, where the headstones and marble angels rose up out of black pumice.

The natives observed the strange behaviour of the visitors, and some of them had enough. The called it an outrage and said that the cemetery would disappear, if the whole town didn't sink into the earth – as when the congregation at Hruna danced itself to the devil on Christmas eve and nothing was ever heard again except howling and yelling from under the ground.

But then natural forces quickly took control and shooed them away with a shower of ashes, fire, and brimstone. People talked a lot about the event afterwards, and pictures of fashion bimbos came out in the newspapers of the capital, with a volcano erupting in the background.

*

Andri sat in the living room with Sara and Howard, where he was having coffee with them after dinner, when a knock came at the door. Sara went to answer it. Andri immediately recognized Kalli's voice.

'Yes, he's here. Won't you come in and have coffee with us?'

Kalli thanked her, took off his boots, and hung up his outer

113

coat.

'Good evening,' he said as he came in with Sara. She offered him a chair.

'Is there any pumice rain?' asked Howard.

'Not in this direction,' Kalli answered and sat down. He had on a turtle-neck sweater.

Sara went into the dining room to get a cup and saucer.

'I was talking to your mother,' Kalli said to Andri.

'I haven't been in touch with her since our house was destroyed.'

'She was somewhat upset and said she hadn't heard from you in a long time. She had seen on television that the house was obviously in great danger. I told her that it was now covered by lava.'

'I've tried many times to call her, but either the line has been busy or she hasn't been there,' Andri responded.

'You don't have to apologize to me for anything . . . .'

Sara brought the coffee.

'You are welcome to call from here if you want to,' said Howard.

'That might be a good idea.'

Howard took him into the office and showed him the phone on the desk next to the window.

Andri sat down in the Consul's old desk chair and started calling. At first it was busy, but finally after many attempts he got through.

He heard that Kalli and Howard had started talking about their attitude toward the International Court of Justice at the Hague.

'I would like Iceland to use the opportunity,' said Howard, 'to present their case in an international forum by sending counsel to defend against the British charges in a trial. Only a very few people know what the dispute is really about.'

'And most people don't give a shit,' said Kalli. 'So we ought

114

to ignore the British and hassle them every way we can. What's this International Court but a club for some old guys who don't know their time is up. Let them just talk to empty chairs in the Hague. They're welcome to it.'

Andri heard his mother called to the telephone.

'I was looking at television tonight and saw pictures of the Islands. My God, it is terrifying to see all the destruction . . . Kalli told me that our house is gone. Why haven't you let me know anything?'

He tried to explain to her his attempts to get in touch with her. Otherwise, nothing else has happened other than what was predictable: the eruption continued and no one knew when or how it might stop.

She said one bright spot was that Parliament had now agreed on a special law to help those who had lost their houses and other property in the eruption on Heimaey. Many good memories were attached to the house and she missed it.

She asked him please to come the next day to visit her. She had an urgent matter to discuss with him.

Kalli and Howard were deep in their discussion when he finished his conversation. He heard Howard say:

'The one universal revolution which has completely succeeded is the jeans revolution, and it came from America like most revolutions.'

Andri needed to go to the bathroom, and he decided to go upstairs rather than to old Ella's toilet down in the cellar, as he was used to doing when he was with Sara.

Also he was curious to see the old bathroom of the Consul's which he had heard so much about.

The bathroom was spacious, and the bathtub itself stood out in the middle of the room. It was unusually long, made of copper which had become very dark, and it rested on lions' feet.

In the corner of the room was a step ladder painted white, with two steps, which the Consul had apparently used when he took a bath.

On the wall was a large mirror in a light-blue frame, and towels hung on bars that were attached to the wall.

This then was where his mother had come to help the old man with his bath after he had stiffened up with arthritis. Or had something else happened between them that she didn't want to talk about, and that had shocked old Ella?

Andri looked around. Yes, there was the wooden bench in the corner on which were thick towels with the monogram of the old Consul's wife embroided in white raised gothic letters.

No, he would not spy on his mother's past, and he hurried back downstairs, as if he had done something immoral.

When he came into the room what did he hear but Howard praising Kalli for his militancy. He said that among all birds and animals there was a sharp class distinction. Those who excelled ruled over the others. And Kalli had indisputable leadership ability. He ought to cultivate it. It didn't matter that he was a little cocky. That was a mark of the leader. It was that way with all the animals most closely related to us, and no one could go against his nature.

Sara offered them more coffee.

Kalli had become almost reticent, but Howard was in high spirits and offered them cognac with their coffee.

At last Kalli stood up to leave.

'Will you be coming too, Andri?'

'Yes, I think so.'

They went into the office. Kalli paused in front of the painting of the Consul.

'Did the old guy have himself buried in this outfit?' he asked sarcastically.

'No, not like that,' Howard answered calmly. 'I even think the Consul's uniform is still here somewhere in the house, little used, if you would be interested in it.'

'Maybe you would like to have yourself buried in it?' asked

116

Sara with an ironic sting in her voice.

'Well, maybe that's not such a crazy idea,' Kalli answered and studied the painting. 'A person should be in some kind of disguise when the time comes.'

'I think there's another costume that would suit you much better,' said Sara.

'Oh – and what costume would that be?' asked Kalli, smiling broadly and putting on his black beret.

'A clown's suit would suit a fool.' Sara's intense black eyes shot sparks.

Kalli burst out in a loud laugh.

'That's the kind of humour I like. Do you hear that, Andri? You ought to try to learn from this humour – it would make you a better poet.'

Howard said something in a friendly tone to Kalli, and Sara motioned to Andri to come with her into the dining room.

She pressed herself hard against him and whispered in a fervent voice, 'Don't be long. I'll wait for you in the cellar. Knock on the window.'

He smelled the scent of her hair and felt her soft body tightly up to his so that tongues of flame entirely enveloped him.

Kalli waited for him in the vestibule.

Howard said goodbye in the doorway. The steps were wet from the rain.

They walked quickly away from the house.

Kalli was angry. His laughter had been only pretence.

'You shouldn't associate with these people. Howard is a dangerous man. He is most assuredly an agent of the Americans. I become more certain of that every time I talk to him.'

*

On the bus out to Vifilstadir the next day Andri went over in his mind the conversation he had had with his mother the

117

evening before.

Why was it so urgent that he visit her? Doubtless she had decided not to return to the Islands, even if the eruption should stop today. Often before she reminded him that Reykjavik was the one place that suited her, she ought to settle there – and hinted with a mysterious smile and searching glances at her son that many opportunities were available to her there.

And Andri remembered the dentist with the horse laugh whom his mother had talked a lot about for a short period of time when her trips to the capital had become very frequent. She said she had gone horseback riding with pleasant people and a ski trip to the Tyrol could have been in the offing – even though she had never been on a pair of skis. And then all of a sudden she stopped talking about the laughing dentist and her shopping trips became infrequent again.

Blended with these reminiscences of his mother and her contacts in the capital were ecstatic currents from the night before and the passionate body of Sara when he had said goodbye to her at daybreak, and almost missed his plane.

All the way in the air he had been in a state of semi-consciousness, yearning only to be in her arms again. He was so numb to what was going on about him that he had failed to notice that the bus was stopped outside the white hospital building and the passengers were pushing toward the door.

Solveig met her son in the entrance hall near the clock and hugged him to her. She took his arm and led him in a motherly fashion up the stairs to the second floor and into the hallway, appearing to be proud of being able to show off her son at her side before the patients.

She opened the door and invited him in. There were two beds made up.

'There are two of us here, but we are both able to get up.'

'How is your asthma feeling?'

'Fine, I could go home, but the chief physician is permitting

118

me to stay until I can adjust to all of the changes – an especially nice man.'

She motioned to her son to sit down in a chair and she herself sat on the edge of the bed.

The beds were against the wall, each on one side of the room, and each with a night table and lamp with a green shade. A larger table was inside the door, with two easy chairs opposite a large clothes press with a mirror. The toilet facilities were down the hall because it was an old building.

On her night table was a half-opened box of candy.

'I didn't bring anything,' he said, 'I was so short of time. I was lucky to catch a flight around noon and just barely caught the bus up here.'

'Bless you, that doesn't make any difference. I have enough candy.' She took the top off the candy box and handed it to him. He took a piece and she took one.

'People are always bringing me candy,' she said meaningfully.

'Haven't the doctors prescribed it for you?'

'No, they certainly don't approve, but I always offer them a piece when they come on rounds – such kindly men and so competent in their profession.'

She sighed and looked at him apologetically.

'If you had become a doctor – and come on rounds in a white coat.'

She looked down with a sad smile.

There was a silence and they heard voices out in the corridor.

'So our house has disappeared under the lava,' she sighed.

'Yes, one of many, and more will be going the same way.'

'What could you save out of it?'

'Almost everything, even your stove.'

'Could you get it – just think of that!'

'There was some junk in the cellar that didn't matter.'

119

'Up in the attic was also an awful lot of stuff.'

Andri nodded his head, 'I collected all that.'

His mother sighed. She looked healthy and plump, her light hair recently done, wearing a blue dress with a gold bracelet and jewelry, a ring with a sea-green turquoise and another with gems in a heart-shaped setting.

'I've met a man here,' she said softly and distinctly, like a school girl who has memorized some rigmarole and recites it at the teacher's desk.

'I've met a man here whom I hope you will like.'

'A doctor?'

'No, he is a patient here like me, something with his heart valves, but he is much better and about to be discharged.'

There was a pause in her speech, and she swallowed.

'This is the first time I have met a man in many years whom I could consider . . . who suits me better than anyone else I have met in many years.'

She stopped and listened. A footstep could be heard outside the door and then a soft knock.

'Come in,' she called.

A tall dark-haired man stood in the doorway, with rough-hewn features and deep lines in his face.

'This is Hannes,' she said.

Andri rose to his feet. They shook hands. The man's hand had black hair and prominent bones.

'Please sit down,' she said.

Hannes took an easy chair by the table and sat a little way from them. He lightly rubbed his nose, which was large, like a hawk's beak. Or was it the eyes that gave him that appearance? He reminds me of a merlin, thought Andri – or even more of a skua.

'Where is Olga?' he asked.

'She must be downstairs. Did the doctor say anything to you about her?'

'It's probably not very good. Wasn't she on blood thinning medicine?'

'What did he say?'

'We can talk about that later,' he answered. 'But what's the latest about the eruption, more and more houses being covered by the lava?'

'Yes, it doesn't look good – '

'We were talking about our house,' said Solveig and smiled affectionately at Hannes.

'Yes, there must be many memories attached to it.'

'Yes, many memories,' she said, 'both happy and sad. Did you see the picture in the paper yesterday, Andri – now where is it?' She looked all about her.

'Isn't this it?' said Hannes and handed her a page from the paper.

'Yes, I knew I had saved it.'

She took it and showed it to her son. It was a picture of Gubbi, broad-shouldered and short-necked, standing by the flag pole on the peak of his new house, which was submerged in black pumice. Under the picture was the caption: The flag flew at half mast for the sinking of his house.

'Yes, Kalli was with him. They went in through a skylight, and it was terrifically hot inside and spraying hot steam,' Andri said.

'Think of it, that splendid new house.'

'But now a law has been passed by Parliament which provides that anyone who suffered loss of property as a result of the eruption in Heimaey can receive full compensation,' said Hannes.

'Hannes's brother is a member of Parliament,' Solveig explained to her son, beaming with pride.

Hannes nodded his head.

'In the law it states that the appropriation shall be for such loss of or disturbance to property as has occurred as a result of volcanic upheavals on Heimaey. It is as unambiguous as could be,' said Hannes.

'Hannes has taken it on himself to research this for me. It is so easy for him on account of his brother. He often goes into Parliament to say hello to him.'

'It's pleasant to go there for coffee,' said Hannes, revealing his large teeth.

'Yes, I heard something about that,' Andri answered, 'they probably stop arguing with each other there, the members of Parliament.'

'They reached unanimity on the bill,' said Hannes and set his brows as though he were recalling the speeches. 'Members from every party understood that such a blow lands not just on those who lost their houses and property in the eruption, but also on the nation as a whole. The government and the opposition were of one mind on the question.'

'Also, in addition to that, contributions have come from home and abroad,' Solveig interjected into the discussion.

Hannes had stood up.

'Wouldn't you like some coffee?' he asked with a cheerful expression after the weighty earnestness.

'Oh yes, we'll come right along,' answered Solveig. 'You go ahead.'

Her plump hand hovered, with its gold rings and lacquered red nails, over the candy box before seizing a piece in pink foil. She looked at them mischievously, her lips pursed while the piece of candy was melting on her tongue.

'You always have such a playful expression when you take a piece of candy,' Hannes said, smiling so broadly that gold teeth were visible behind the ones in front.

'That is because I am always stealing—it's so much fun for me to steal.' She laughed so that dimples appeared in her cheeks.

'And not one piece of candy more,' said Hannes, raising his

index finger at her threateningly.

He had a large gold ring with a reddish brown stone.

Gaiety danced in her eyes.

'I've ordered coffee for the three of us and graham crackers for you, Solla,' he said, nodding to them as he turned in the doorway.

They heard his footsteps move away from the door.

'We amuse ourselves like this every day,' she said, beaming after the successful introductions. 'I don't know how I could have endured it here without him, and he also plays the piano so well.'

'Is he a pianist?'

'Oh no, he is a ship broker, but he often plays for me in the evening when the patients are staring at some television series. There are hit tunes from the old days and all kinds of songs – he's terribly musical.

'What kind of ring does he have on his finger?'

'Some kind of signet ring, I think. His father was a goldsmith.'

'A ship broker with a signet ring,' Andri said as if to himself.

'He often goes abroad to buy ships.'

She started to talk about her plans for the future, that she would sell the book stock and stop running the shop. Now she had something a little different in mind and could benefit from Hannes's help, who knew all the ropes and had a brother who was in Parliament and on all kinds of committees.

'We got his tickets the other day to an opening at the National Theatre because he couldn't go himself. It was a wonderful evening. We got something to eat down in The Cellar and had red wine with it. Hannes took a long time choosing just the right year for us. It was first-class service. And then afterwards we went to the bar at Naust for a little while. Don't you think it's different to live such a life? It suits me so well. Of course I was feeling so rotten the first days here, really the first two weeks, that I had to be on tranquilizers, and then I met Hannes and he saved me. I think that in some way we understand each other so well, yes I should just say it right out: that I think I have never known a man – for many years now – who has been so agreeable to me.'

'You may have said that at times before,' Andri said softly.

'I? When?'

'I can't remember precisely.'

'No wonder, because I haven't done it. He is the one man since your father died. . . .'

The words died on her lips.

'You aren't opposed to him like . . . ?'

'No, he is entirely different from Keli.'

'He is terribly popular here in the sanitarium – and sometimes spends time down in the lounge with the doctors. His brother the M.P. was in school with the chief physician.'

'How old is he?'

'Somewhat older than me.'

'Yes, it seemed so to me.'

'But a few years don't matter when people are suited to each other.'

'Are you thinking about getting married then?'

'Yes, maybe, I hope you aren't jealous.' She rubbed her short fingers lightly on his cheek. 'You know that nothing could come between us, never.'

'No, of course you live your life and I live mine.'

'Yes,' she agreed a little sadly, 'we have been too dependent on each other, but that is because you were all I had.'

'Your sweetheart is probably getting impatient waiting for you,' Andri said standing up.

He wasn't eager to hear his mother's analysis of her emotions.

'That's true, we shouldn't make him wait too long.' She

stood up.

'You want us then to sell all the book stock just as it is,' said Andri, as he walked out of the room behind her.

'Yes, but we can talk about that better later, after I have left here, which will be very soon.'

They met the patients on the stairs coming back from coffee.

Hannes stood up from the table when they came into the room and adjusted her chair with great courtesy before she sat down. She chose a seat where she was protected from the bright late-winter light coming through the large windows. Snow squalls competed with bright reflections of the sun among dark clouds.

A lame woman came up to their table and greeted Solveig with a handshake.

'I though that was you, Solla dear,' said the lame woman, 'isn't that your son?'

Solveig off-handedly introduced them both to her, but when the woman began to recount her medical history Solveig interrupted, saying that she wanted to talk to her later, but that her son was on a very short visit.

The woman gave an embarrassed smile and limped toward the door.

'Who is she?' whispered Hannes. 'She must have just come.'

'She's called Gauja. We lived out in the east at the same time. They were horribly poor and Daddy was always trying to help them.'

'He couldn't have made much money that way,' said Hannes, taking a piece of Christmas cake with large raisins in it.

'No, Daddy never looked at things that way, but he did have enough worries of his own, with a house full of children. And yet he had his prerogatives.'

'You mean the barber shop,' her son corrected her.

'That couldn't have been a goldmine,' said Hannes.

125

'No, what I said was correct. He had prerogatives. He sold various things to a certain extent and he had the herring salting in the summer.'

'And all the daughters in salt,' Hannes said and blinked his eyes at her.

'Yes, of course we helped with the herring salting. We were terribly strictly brought up. Daddy sometimes locked us sisters in the house when the sailors were all ashore and a dance was advertised in the community hall.'

'But you escaped anyway,' said Hannes with an indulgent smile and teasing eyes.

Solveig laughed.

'I remember we sneaked out to a dance once and Daddy completely lost control of himself, and then Mama came and rescued us. She always had such a good way with Daddy.'

'It is no wonder that he would get a little upset . . . .'

'Hannes, you shouldn't tease me,' she whined, and then laughed. 'Because it's true what I say. Mama had also had so much discipline at home—she had in some sense been raised in an archdeacon's home, and was such a great lady . . . .'

Andri listened to his mother recollecting old stories from her youth, which he had heard countless times and had long since stopped putting his full faith in.

After coffee she wanted the men to go for a stroll, although the weather was not the best. For herself she said she wasn't up to it.

They walked east along the building and down to the lake. The ground was mostly clear, although there were patches of snow on slopes and in ditches. Two ravens came over the hill croaking and bustling about. The lake was partly covered with ice and further out were open holes in the ice which the wind rippled. A barbed wire fence went all the way down to the shore, and on the other side stood some shaggy horses with their backs to the weather.

126

'It's an indication of the bad weather how the horses stand,' said Hannes. 'It should be coming out of the northwest.'

The horses sauntered over to them when they got to the fence and reached out their noses.

'They're hungry,' said Hannes.

'Yes, that's the way these big shots take care of their horses,' said Andri and was reminded of the dentist that his mother had sent him to in Reykjavik on credit. He had refused to go back to him.

They looked over the frozen peat ridges and solitary tufts of dead grass on the hillock.

'There are no scraps here.'

'The best thing would be to let them out through the fence,' said Andri.

'I don't see a gate anywhere near here.' Hannes ran his eyes along the fence.

'Should we go further?' he asked.

'Where to?'

'We would have to climb over the fence.'

They turned and went back the way they had come.

'Your mother is a great heroine,' Hannes said when they had got back to the gate into the sanitarium grounds.

'Heroine? How is that?'

'I don't mean Bergthora.'

'Or Hallgerdur?'

'No, a modern heroine. I have great respect for her. It has been a difficult time for her.'

'Are you planning to go back to the University?' asked Hannes.

'Play school would be just as good a name for it.'

'Hadn't you advanced a long way into medicine?'

'No one gets a long way into medicine.'

'I understood that from your mother.'

'Yes, Mama . . . .'

'I think you can make good money from it.'

'I thought you were the chief physician when you came in before.'

'Did you think so?'

A low chortle of satisfaction came from Hannes against a gust of wind.

'Yes, the thought entered my mind briefly.'

People were drifting out toward the bus when they came into the entrance hall.

'There is another bus after about an hour,' said Solveig – 'or you could come back tomorrow – yes, please do that.'

He promised to. They went out into the snow squall. His mother wore a light woollen scarf over her hair, in which some tiny pieces of snow caught and melted as she stood half shivering by the bus.

The driver, with a leather bag in front of him, collected the fares as the passengers stepped into the long dark carriage.

Solveig and Hannes stood in the open door of the sanitarium and waved to Andri when the bus moved around the circular driveway.

*

Andri stayed over night at his aunt Gústa's on the west side of town, as he had done so often when he came to the capital with his mother.

Now the children had left home and it was roomier than it used to be in the little stone house belonging to Ragnar the warehouseman.

It was dark by the time he rang her doorbell.

She was as cheerful as ever, with laughing brown eyes and dark hair that was beginning to show some grey.

He apologized for not having let her know he was coming, but she said that a bed was always made up for him to use

128

whenever he wished, night or day.

He only had one hand-bag, which he had been able to leave during the day with a friend of his in the dormitory.

She would hear of nothing else but that he have coffee with her, though he told her he had just finished coffee with his mother up at Vifilsstadir.

'Yes, sister Solla visited the other day. She showed me the new one she has such a crush on. There's nothing like the way she is always in love. She is perpetually young in that respect.'

'And yourself?'

'I?' she giggled and laughed. 'No, I've never loved anyone but my Raggi, even if other people might not have found him exciting.'

She asked about Hannes and how Andri had liked him.

'He's a little like a bird of prey,' said Andri, 'that big nose and the eyes.'

'Yes, I see what you mean – eagle-like?'

'Maybe he's more like a Pigeon Hawk or – ?'

Gústa laughed.

'But he's a fine type,' she said. 'He's separated and has grown-up children, so that's all right, but he has been living with another woman for many years. It looks like that is down the drain now.'

Andri drank his coffee quietly in the kitchen with her as she went on chattering. She was making paté.

'I think he likes to have a good time,' she continued, 'and goes out a lot to restaurants with the woman he lives with, who is very rich.'

She laughed again. Her cheerfulness put everyone around her in a good mood, except Ragnar, who at just this moment came home from work.

He said hello to Andri in a friendly manner and started asking him about the eruption, and what the outlook was.

Andri told him that he was afraid that the harbour would be

129

sealed off, but then the possibility arose of breaking through the Isthmus into the harbour, because as bad as it would be to have the entrance sealed, the harbour itself was very valuable, not just for the Westman Islanders but for the whole of the South, which was essentially without a harbour.

'Where are you going to get the money for that?' called Ragnar from the bathroom, where he was washing himself.

'Money!' cried out Gústa, 'Ragnar dear, there's always enough money in Iceland.' She giggled.

'It would cost billions.'

'What's a billion?' she teased her husband.

'And it would have to be found in the pockets of us tax payers. We would be expected to pay for the whole thing,' Ragnar called over the sound of the running water.

'It is a loss to the whole nation,' said Andri.

'Nation, what nation?' Ragnar asked, and came into the kitchen bare-chested. He had red spots on his white neck and shoulders.

'This isn't a nation,' he said, 'Icelanders aren't a nation. They are nothing but pressure groups, each one against the others.'

'Raggi dear, it's in all the textbooks that Iceland is a more than one-thousand-year-old nation.'

'It's all the same to me what's in the textbooks. Who wrote them?'

'You've bought them for your children.'

Ragnar huffed.

'Here's your cup, dear,' said Gústa and handed him a brown mug. Ragnar took it without drinking the coffee.

'They're going to use the volcanic eruption as a pretext for increasing taxes, in order to disguise their inability to govern the country.'

'But it's a leftist government now,' said Andri calmly.

Ragnar was sipping from his mug and almost choked.

'A leftist government with the same old conservative solutions: devaluation and wage controls. We wage earners should have received a six percent increase according to agreements, but now it's all gone into social security and into keeping exports high. . . .'

'Now, now, Raggi dear, just drink your coffee in peace. It never turns out as bad as it looks,' Gústa soothed her husband.

'We don't have them to thank for it,' said Ragnar sipping from his mug again.

'How has the salvage work gone with you otherwise?' he asked, having now regained his temper.

'Pretty well. Things have been saved from most of the houses before they were buried by ash or burned.'

'I have heard disgraceful stories about that. All this rescue work done in a terrible rush and panic,' Ragnar continued, 'and millions of kronas worth of home appliances ruined.'

'Yes, that may be so, if the location were difficult for getting appliances out of the houses. It still remains to salvage the most expensive equipment if it keeps going this way,' Andri said.

Ragnar went back to the bathroom.

'He's often this way when he comes home from work,' Gústa said in confidence. 'He always lets himself get worked up by politics.'

'And other property worth hundreds of millions,' Ragnar called from the bathroom.

They could hear him huffing and gasping for breath under the taps in the sink.

'More coffee?' said Gústa with the coffee pot in the air, pouring it into Andri's cup before he had time to object.

Ragnar was drying himself with a towel back in the hallway.

'They are tickled to death to have this eruption in order to deny us our contractual rights.'

'But the experts say that this is not the time for wage increases and making demands,' said Andri, who couldn't resist teasing Ragnar a little.

'Experts! Do you call them experts?' said Ragnar worn down. He went back to the couple's bedroom.

Gústa began asking Andri about the number of houses that had been destroyed. He told her that their house had been covered by lava.

Ragnar came back into the kitchen in a clean shirt, but his hair was still wet.

'Did you know that their house was covered by lava?'

He hadn't heard that.

'And you think they shouldn't get any compensation? It wasn't their fault.'

'Yes, of course they should get compensation, but we aren't the ones that should pay them, but the insurance companies, which have raked in the profits without any thought of the public welfare.'

Ragnar sat with them on a stool. He had finished letting off steam for the moment, and they talked together calmly about everyday matters.

Later in the evening they saw pictures of the eruption on the news. There were countless pipes and hoses from pumping ships up on the high face of the lava and two bulldozers in action.

The newsman said that the lava had got to the harbour wall over a fifteen metre distance, but the geologists that he talked to maintained that without the cooling with seawater, dozens of houses would have been covered by lava in the eastern part of town, where undamaged houses still stood, and the harbour would likely have been sealed shut without it. The main consideration was to get more powerful pumps and larger pipes for the seawater cooling, and to deliver them to that location.

Afterwards came pictures of Olof Palme, the prime minister of Sweden, getting out of an airplane at Keflavik airport.

'We regret that we could not support Iceland in the matter of territorial waters that is before the United Nations,' Palme said on his arrival. 'We understand the Icelandic point of view, but our policy is to await the decision of the International Court before we take a direct position on your dispute.'

'Obviously the Swedes don't give a damn about us Icelanders – we aren't yellow or black,' said Ragnar.

And they kept on watching television.

*

When Andri came back to visit his mother the next day, Hannes had needed to run an errand in town, so the two of them were alone during the whole visit.

She told him that she had now decided to marry Hannes within a few weeks. They would go on a honeymoon to Italy, set up a new home in Reykjavik, and in the autumn open a shop selling objets d'art in Hannes's father's old place, a goldsmith's shop he had owned for many years just off Laugavegur.

He listened to what she said without expressing his own opinion.

Finally she directed her talk to himself. She said she heard he had got into the habit of spending time at the Consul's house.

'Have you and Howard got to be such good friends?' she asked.

'No, it's mainly Sara that I have been visiting.'

'Oh, what is she doing there?'

'She came to the Islands to fetch old Ella, but she doesn't want to abandon the Consul's house, so Sara has stayed on.'

'I hope there is nothing between you two,' she said as if warning him.

'No, just the usual.'

'Meaning?' She looked with panic at her son.

'You're always whining at me that I should get to know a girl, and now I've done it.'

'Her father has had so much trouble over her.'

133

'That has all been blown out of proportion.'

'No, there is so much mental illness in her family.'

'There's mental illness in all families.'

'It's not just for that reason.'

'But for?'

Solveig bit her lip and sighed deeply.

'There are so many.'

'She's the daughter of this man that you . . . .'

'That is the reason exactly – oh I don't know how I should say it.'

She squeezed her hands together until her knuckles turned white.

'I've always hoped that it would never need to come to this : . . .'

'I don't care what you say about her, it makes no difference. You should really be happy that it's turned out I'm not gay.'

'That never occurred to me.'

'Yes it did, try not to lie to yourself, or to me. You've often mentioned it, and I had even been half afraid of that myself, but now I know better.'

'Do you love her?' Her eyes were round and questioning.

'Love? I can't stand that word. It is so worn out and over used. I can't make myself say it, but she is the woman who lets me enjoy myself – in bed, if more explanation is required.'

'But that must never happen.'

'What?'

'You must not sleep with her.'

'Who can forbid it?'

'It's against the law of nature.'

Andri gave a short laugh. 'I thought that it was exactly in accordance with nature's law.'

'She's your half-sister.'

'My half-sister? What craziness.'

'Well, it's true. I swear to you it's true.'

She lay the palm of her right hand on her heart.

'Are you trying to tell me that I am Frimann's son?'

His mother had grown very pale.

'Yes, you are,' she sighed, 'he is your father.'

'Some people believe rather that I am the son of the Consul,' Andri let slip.

'Oh, you must not say that, you hurt me so deeply,' sighed his mother, 'there was never any sexual connection between the old man and me. He was too decrepit to perform that way with me.'

'But you have perhaps performed that way on him.'

Andri looked at his mother, panic stricken and helpless in a chair there before him, with her golden ornaments and trinkets, the bright red lipstick dried on her lips.

He remembered incidents from long ago, when the Consul would take him to the glass cabinet and show him his bird collection. How he had gazed in fascination at the king eider with his common eiders, who bowed their heads to him. He had something like a crown on his head. And ever since he thought of the Consul as an eider king in his nesting ground and his mother as one of the eiders, perhaps the youngest and most eager.

He heard his mother explain that she had never been the Consul's mistress, although she had sometimes helped him in the bathtub because he had become so stiff and had difficulty scrubbing his back. But there was never anything physical between them. That was nothing but malicious gossip. The most he had done was maybe pat her or stroke her, but it never went any further.

'But wasn't Frimann in America all that time? How could he. . .?'

'Oh don't torment me with these questions,' she pleaded. 'Open the window, I am feeling so ill.'

She breathed deeply, her cheeks burning and her eyes glow-

135

ing.

'I can't avoid asking when you tell me such a thing. . . .'

Andri opened the window just a crack. It was calm weather and not much below freezing. The sound of hammers came from the extension below.

'Frimann came to the Islands for several days the summer before you were born,' his mother said in the slow manner of reminiscence. 'Your dad was fishing for herring in the north and I worked at the reception desk in the hotel, sometimes into the night. It was Midsummer and bright the whole night and before I knew it Frimann stood in front of me one evening, and I didn't know but that he was somewhere in America, where he had been for so long. No one was there, and red sunbeams streamed into the mirror above the counter. I couldn't say anything I was so amazed and he just said: 'I've come to find you, where can we go?''

'Nothing else?'

'No, nothing else. . . .'

She recalled how he had taken her hand and right away it was if she were in a trance and let him lead her up the stairs, into the hallway in the attic, to the room that she could use, and a bed awaited them. . . .

She recalled how all the words and the accusations against Frimann, which she had thought about him so often and for so long, gathered together like a lump in her throat, without her getting them out, and before she knew it she had let him undress her in the soft dusk of midnight, and she seized his curly head as though it were a treasure of gold which she had recovered from a sunken wreck on the ocean's floor, and she had still not uttered any word but pressed it against her bare breast, and he never got to hear of all her impatience, waiting for years on end in merciless silence. She was again in the control of the ancient sorcery which made them speechless in the body's pleasure and it was not before he had left and the roar of her blood had

136

subsided again into her veins that she remembered the words she had intended to hurt him with like sharp blades.

'We met one night, no, really two nights, but I never told your dad about it and no one ever knew that we had met.'

'And it was then that I. . . ?'

'Yes, it was then.'

'Did Frimann know about it?'

'No, I never spoke to him again after those nights, maybe there were three of them. Never. I wanted to forget what happened because he had treated me so badly, but I did hope he would be unhappy with his American wife, because she never could have loved him as I did. Yes, you are right to blame me, condemn me for being so pliable, but I did not create myself.'

'And Dad never discovered how it was?'

'No, never, and he never suspected anything. He came home from the herring before the season was over because the fishing was so poor. I had stopped having my period, but he didn't know anything about that, and so you were on the way and everything was entirely normal, and we were so joyful with you when you were born, and you got the best father in the world, if he had only been allowed to live . . . .'

Her voice broke and she took up a little lace handkerchief and blew her nose quietly.

'That can't be right,' Andri murmured, 'it's just fantasy and wishful thinking.'

'No, it's the truth, the greatest truth in my life. You are also a little like Frimann when you look closer.'

'Some people might trace that straight back to the Consul.'

'Oh Andri, why do you try to hurt me? I don't deserve it. I tried to resist him those midsummer nights, although I couldn't. I've also heard that those are sorcerers' nights.'

She pulled herself to him and tried to kiss him.

'I had to tell you this to prevent you from committing incest with your half-sister. Vengeance could be brought on you for

137

that, because it is against the law of God and man. You could
have a half-wit or God knows what. It must not happen. You
must stop seeing her.'

'I won't. I can't do that any more than you could yourself on
those nights.'

'I will tell her then.'

'Sara would only laugh at you.'

'You must do it, or else I will believe it is the punishment of
God.'

He felt her embrace just as in the old days when she had
come home late and he had waited for her awake in the bed
unable to sleep, and then she came in to him, sat on the side of
the bed and kissed him with wet and slippery kisses and it stayed
for a long time afterwards in his nostrils, this unknown bodily
odour that had accompanied her.

On the way in the bus he thought about how Sara might take
it if he told her what had happened to him.

Wouldn't she think his mother was really deranged, wanting
to blame a dead man for a child conceived so long ago?

But even if he kept quiet about it all, would he himself be
able to continue his relationship with her, untroubled by suspicion – even certainty – which would not leave him in peace.

*

Flights to the Islands were cancelled for the next few days on
account of the weather, and Andri could with a good conscience
hang around town as he used to, meeting his friends in coffee
houses, going to movies and libraries, listening to music and
looking through the book stores. It seemed to him that he had
been away from Reykjavik much longer than he really had. But
he had to go back—anything else was out of the question as long
as Sara was still there. Besides which, he needed to do some
things for his mother.

On the flight back he was with some scientists who were

doing research on the eruption and some foreign specialists.

He was told that one of them was a world famous volcanist who had been sent to the country by the United Nations.

The sea was rough and grey below them, and the plane began to toss about when they came in over the island.

The scientists tried to point the volcano out to the expert. It was mostly hidden by dark clouds of smoke and white billows of steam. But when the plane descended it was easy to see the black expanse of lava on the island, covering the slopes of the new mountain and overrunning the easternmost part of the town all the way to the harbour wall. Then came rows of houses at the edge of the lava, straight streets and small houses with attics and dormers, and larger buildings, schools and a hospital building, as if everything were going on as usual.

But it quickly turned out to be all otherwise as they drove down in the airline bus from the airport into the half-submerged and deserted town: all life departed, windows like empty eyes, nowhere children at play, nowhere women chatting, nowhere productive life, nothing except men shovelling coal-black ash from the roofs of houses.

In halting English, Dr. Tazieff the volcanist told about his experience with the eruption of Etna, where he had worked at the request of the Italian government. There the lava had been lightly flowing, with a possibility therefore of using explosives to direct the course of the lava flow; but it came to nothing because the grape farmers on the mountain slopes killed the idea. The result was that the lava flow ran unhindered over the vineyards and orchards, so that everything was buried in lava and all signs of human habitation destroyed.

The pumping ships outside the harbour and the seawater cooling were pointed out to him, but he shook his head and said that it was worthless. He had himself tried it on Etna without any result.

They drove down to the hotel where the passenger terminal

139

was and from there up to the site of the eruption.

A geologist described to Dr. Tazieff how the mountain had piled up around the crater until the edges were equal in height, and then the edge that in some part faced the town began to sink forward and it had continued in that direction for a half a kilometre, obliquely toward the town, and in that area all the buildings had already been buried under ash. At that point the mountain subsided and the eruption itself had somewhat diminished in recent days and the flow of lava was northeast toward the sea, although side branches running west toward the highest guard wall were noticeable. People had built a new road in that direction to replace the other one covered by lava, and used bulldozers to build up a guard wall, though it was apparent to everyone that walls did not have much effect when the lava slid forward with the force of hell.

Pipes lay from the harbour most of the way up the hillside, and firemen directed the nozzles wherever they could spot a lava ember or a sign of burning.

Howard, who was in the party with the volcanist, told him that they would try to get special pipes from Texas that were used in oil work and could carry many times more than the pipes they used now, but the doctor answered that it wouldn't be of any help.

When it was pointed out to him that the movement of lava in the direction of the harbour entrance seemed to have stopped because of the seawater cooling, he said that other conditions were responsible.

After supper in the middle-school cafeteria, a meeting was called with the volcano scientist.

Dr. Tazieff, a slender, rather short man, with a large nose on his sun-tanned face, looked over the group who had taken seats in the school room in front of the high writing desk that stood next to him.

He picked up some chalk and began to draw on the

blackboard. First he drew the island like a rock coming up out of the ocean. The island stood on a mountain peak which had formed out of the ocean bottom on the earth's crust. He drew a thickness of the earth's crust of sixty or seventy kilometres, below which came a layer of basalt 1,500 degrees hot that had made its way through the thick earth's crust and up through the mountain on the island until it let itself go in this eruption, which was destroying the inhabited area of the island.

'No human power can resist this awesome expulsion from the bowels of the earth, coming from such a depth,' said Dr. Tazieff, and took some water to drink after finishing this introduction.

Thin hair barely hid his light brown bald spot.

'Nothing will do here but to be realistic,' he continued, setting the water glass down. 'It must inevitably be acknowledged that the town is doomed, and that the only question is when it will give its last gasp. The ash fall can produce a slow demise, burying the town in the next two months if the wind direction is unfavourable – or it could happen quite suddenly.'

People were obviously shocked at such an unconditional death sentence over the community they had tried for many weeks to save, and had persuaded themselves that they had to some extent succeeded in doing.

The doctor pointed out that the eruption on Surtsey had lasted for four years and that it was highly probable this eruption would behave in a manner similar to that one.

'So I will warn you of the danger that gas is an indication of,' he continued. 'The island will clearly rise like a soufflé. Metre long fissures have been found in lava only a few days old and similar fissures can be hidden under ash deposits in the town. Gas is extremely lethal, as the rat killing in the cellars of houses is irrefutable testimony of. The great danger to human beings cannot be emphasized strongly enough.'

He took another drink from the glass of water and his

Adam's apple was very noticeable when he swallowed.

'The gas can also indicate that other eruptions might occur in the middle of the town,' he continued. 'The city could then disappear under flowing lava and billions of tons of ash in a few hours.'

There was an infectious silence. No one in the audience made a sound. It was as if the rumbling from the volcano had doubled in volume. He resumed his speech. 'The temperature of the gas is one of the indicators that volcanists use in predicting the behaviour of volcanoes, and for that reason it is necessary to observe it with precision and to move people away immediately if it begins to rise.'

After the volcano specialist had finished his talk, people seemed to be exhausted by this ominous description of the situation, and they just stared forward deep in thought. Then an Icelandic scientist rose from his seat and spoke in Icelandic.

He said that this seemed prematurely pessimistic to him.

'Here at home we know this kind of gas from the Hekla eruptions,' he said, 'and in general it is a sign that the eruption is on the decline. The formation of gas is more likely to indicate narrowing of the crater than danger of a new eruption. Of course time alone will tell whether that is so in this case, but as long as it does not heat up in the borehole here on the west side of town, I cannot believe that another eruption is imminent.'

The participants in the meeting were greatly relieved at these words of the scientist, whom everyone knew to have had a great deal of experience with eruptions in Iceland. Then speaking in English, he addressed his words to Dr. Tazieff, telling of his observations of Hekla eruptions and Surtsey.

Several geologists also began to speak, and the meeting did not end until long into the night.

Dr. Tazieff did not get to Reykjavik, and he had to spend the night in the town. Because of overcrowding in the hotel, he was put up in the Maritime Museum.

Later, he himself described the night to reporters in Reykjavik: 'We slept on the floor in a large room with twelve lighted fish tanks. There was an uncanny yellow light that seemed like the underworld. During the night while the mountain erupted and rumbled we saw the fish swim towards us and open their jaws, revealing many rows of sharp teeth in the monsters. I couldn't sleep much. I have never spent another night like it – and have no wish to repeat it.'

*

Andri had hoped that he would see Sara at the meeting with the volcano scientist, but she did not appear there, and he did not get a chance to talk to Howard either, even though he was in the group around Dr. Tazieff.

He went to the cafeteria later in the evening to have a look around for her, but she wasn't there either.

It was close to midnight. Grimur the lighthouse keeper had given a reading in the cafeteria for the firemen. It was a new poem about the British, and had been well received.

He called the poem *Lullaby for the British*. It was composed in the style of the *Lullaby for the Turks*, which had been written centuries ago when people were most terrified of the Algerian pirates after their raids on the Islands.

Grimur adapted the *Lullaby for the Turks* to the archenemy British, whom the Icelanders would defeat by sending ghosts and revenants after them.

The lads enthusiastically praised Grimur the lighthouse keeper's poetic mastery, and said that if someone were going to appear in the International Court in the Hague on behalf of the Icelanders, to answer the complaint of the British, it ought to be Grimur the lighthouse keeper, who would silence them with poetry.

Grimur was triumphant, and Kalli chided Andri for allowing the old fellow to excel so completely as a war poet.

'I went to the Consul's house one day while you were away,' said Kalli and puffed on his pipe with a coffee mug in front of him.

'And?'

'I had a suspicion that Howard agreed with the articles in the Reykjavik afternoon papers which demanded that the Americans be asked to provide equipment and pipes for the seawater cooling.'

'Did you ask him about it?'

'I did, but he never answers directly, that man. But of course a government which considers itself to be leftist could not seek assistance from the Americans—it would be impossible.'

'Did you stay long?'

'No, they were a little surprised at my coming—they had been smoking hash.'

'No, that can't be.'

'Do you think I don't know the smell of hash? For two years I was on welfare in Copenhagen and lived for a while in Kristiania.'

'Did you have any with them?'

'No, no, they hid it from me, and besides Sara had just come out of the bath. She was barefoot in her bathrobe.'

'She could hardly have been smoking in the bath.'

'I don't know what they do in that family, but people say they are big on taking baths.'

Kalli grinned.

'The same cannot be said of some others,' Andri answered curtly.

'Why do you think Howard didn't invite the volcano scientist to stay with him? It was because he wanted to be undisturbed with Sara.'

Andri sprang to his feet. Kalli laughed.

'Don't play the lovelorn nightingale, that won't work in this situation,' Kalli called to him.

144

But Andri had rushed to the door.

He was unaware until he was most of the way to the Consul's house of the direction he had taken.

It was pitch dark, no moon, no stars and no light in the windows of the Consul's house.

It was as if the house had contracted, wishing to expose as little of itself as possible there in the dark. The windows looked full of mystery.

He stood some distance away and listened for a sound, but there was nothing except the fluttering of a sheet of tin that had come loose in the wind. Otherwise dead silence.

He turned from the house and hurried away.

When he got home he threw himself down in his lair and tried to sleep in his clothes, but that strange noise began to sound more and more like the whispering of lovers, and it kept him awake for a long time, uneasy in his heart.

*

The ridge which had split from the volcano continued to move closer to the harbour. It seemed to push forward ahead of a wall of flowing lava deep beneath all the solidified weight. In places it cut through the lava like an iceberg through surface ice.

The news went around that the old water pipes, which had been put into service after the new ones were destroyed, had suffered the same fate and broken apart on the ocean floor. Now people had to use emergency water from an old well, but it was impure and undrinkable.

The lava pushed the barrier walls ahead of it and over onto houses and buildings, so there wasn't even time for them to burn.

People tried to pump seawater on the edges of the lava and wherever thin-flowing streams appeared, but it didn't seem to have any effect, the progress of the lava was unstoppable.

In one spurt the firemen lost both hoses and pumps under the lava flow and had to run for their lives.

A great deal of attention was given to saving the electric power station. A huge barrier wall had been pushed up in a semi-circle around it, which in the event proved to be of little use as the lava face inched forward step by step with a metallic creaking that had succeeded in getting on people's nerves, and the lava wave flowed up to the walls of the station.

The workers were obstinate about leaving the engines, even when the window panes were beginning to break because of the heat, and it was not until large cracks appeared in the masonry walls, threatening to collapse them under the weight and pressure of the molten lava that the engines were shut down and the workmen left the engine room in sulphur fumes and clouds of steam.

Immediately all electricity went out, and there was no light in the darkened town except from volcanic fires and burning houses.

There was no opportunity to salvage the generator, which was almost new and a very valuable piece of equipment. The forward movement of the lava was greater than people had expected and the generator disappeared under glowing lava boulders in a short time. After the generator was destroyed an attempt was made to use an auxiliary engine which could still produce electricity for minimal usage.

The whole time until then, the capelin processing had been going on with only brief interruptions, but now the end had come because of the power outage, and also with the approach of spring the capelin had largely left the fishing grounds.

The next day the flare-up began to subside and the lava flow seemed to have stopped.

People exerted themselves once more, laying new pipes out on the lava, but inquiries to Scandinavia and Holland about sufficiently powerful pumps and larger pipes had not borne results.

Andri had stayed in the uncomfortable book shop. There was no heat in the furnace because he had forgotten to turn off the water before he went to visit his mother and the pipes had burst in his absence, as had occurred widely in the unoccupied houses, and he had not been able to get them repaired.

One evening he determined to wait no longer to meet Sara because she would not allow herself to be seen. He walked out Shore Road after he had washed and changed his clothes.

It was getting dark out and there were not any street lights since the power station went under the lava. He felt his heart pounding heavily and thought at first that it was from the anticipation of seeing Sara again, but when he began to have trouble breathing he realized that it came from gas poisoning, which the police had warned about in low-lying places and in the cellars of houses.

He walked faster and when he got to the Consul's house the effect was completely gone.

It was quickly growing dark and no lights were on except Ella's down in the cellar. He went up the steps and knocked on the door and waited some time to hear any sound from inside, but it was silent as a tomb and he knocked again. Finally he tried the door bell although he knew for sure that it was out of order, and again he tried knocking on the door, to no effect.

Finally he went down to the cellar door and knocked there at the old woman's.

Footsteps approached and a key was turned in the lock.

Old Ella opened the door half-way and called out.

'Who is it?'

Andri said it was he.

'What do you want?'

He asked whether Sara was at home.

'No, she's asleep.'

'Couldn't I talk to her?'

'She's sleeping,' repeated the old woman grumpily and

started to close the door.

'Is she ill?'

'Yes,' answered the old women and slammed the door shut.

He stood outside and heard her drag her feet down the hallway and slam the inner door after her. Wouldn't Sara have awakened with this rough door slamming? But he heard no sound from inside the house.

The sound of the surf from the Isthmus to the west boomed against the rumbling from the volcano.

What was going on? Were they practising sorcery together and calling forth spirits from the land of the dead as had happened before in this house?

Andri recalled the story about the old woman's powers as a medium when she was young, always with that uncanny transparent look in her eyes which seemed to see through heights and hills and to perceive events in other dimensions than normal human sight.

In those years the Consul had locked himself in with Ella who went into a trance and wrote automatically for him, her handwriting varying from a primitive scrawl to a cultivated script.

The Consul sought advice for every kind of occurrence in the family, such as his wife's ill health, which she did not succeed in following, ending her days in a clinic out in Denmark.

During the night he dreamed the same dream many times. He thought he was with Sara out in the black wreckage of a ship, and suddenly the sea began to get rough and to rise. They intended to get out of there, but became separated, and finally when he had succeeded in getting to land he discovered to his great dismay that Sara was still behind in the wreckage, which the angry sea was covering over.

He saw the surf rush over the wreckage, submerging it, and awoke sweaty, with the heavy sound of the surf, which was in reality the booming of the volcano.

148

The next day was bright and fair, with no noticeable flow of lava toward the harbour.

The firemen laboured out on the lava to lay new pipes and people began again to regain their optimism.

The lava face seemed to have halted at a building of Isborg that offered a great deal of resistance, constructed of reinforced concrete. But the lava had run down into the cisterns, and the salthouse was entirely destroyed.

Howard went out on the lava to where the firemen were working feverishly to set up a new defence system.

He gave them the news that officials had finally agreed to accept the pipes and pumps from the United States that had been a standing offer, after a long squabble in a closed cabinet meeting.

Five C 52-A cargo planes departed from New York en route to Keflavik with large and powerful equipment.

Andri asked Howard how Sara was. He wondered what he meant, not seeming to know that anything was wrong with her.

'Old Ella told me that she was ill,' said Andri and tried to conceal his surprise at this inconsistency among members of the household.

'Oh yes, of course, she had a touch of gas poisoning, but I thought she was completely recovered. Maybe we should send both the old woman and Sara to Reykjavik because of the danger of gas,' Howard said with a serious expression.

Then in the evening Andri went back to the Consul's house and knocked on the door. Quick footsteps were audible inside and Howard came to the door.

'Andri,' he said, 'come in. It's some time since we've had a game of chess.'

'I don't know whether I am in the mood for chess now,' said Andri and walked ahead of him into the office.

In the living room sat Sara, putting a record on the turntable.

The air was thick with the smoke of Gaulois cigarettes.

Andri said to himself that was certainly what Kalli had taken to be the smell of hashish, though he would not have been willing to admit it.

Sara made an indistinct sound in her throat when she saw who had come into the living room toward her.

'I've been trying to get in touch with you, with no luck,' he said softly.

Howard had not come into the room.

'Yes?' she said brusquely and seemed to be a bit surprised.

'We were having a drop of cognac with coffee,' Howard said, indicating the coffee table where cups and liqueur glasses stood. 'Won't you join us?'

'Yes, please, thank you.'

Andri's eyes still rested on Sara, on her dark hair, which flowed over her shoulders and billowed like glistening kelp when she moved her head.

'I'll get a cup,' said Howard and went into the dining room.

Sara started the record and lit a cigarette. Andri picked up a cognac glass and poured into it from the slender-necked bottle.

Howard came with a cup and saucer from the dining room cupboard and poured from the thermos flask into his cup. They sat down and listened to the Beatles sing 'Help, I need somebody . . . .'

After the song ended they continued to sit as though they were listening, but the only sound was the rumbling of the volcano.

Finally Howard said, 'Six cargo planes have come to Keflavik with high-pressure pumps, pipes of the right size and other equipment from the United States.'

Andri nodded his head absent-mindedly. He wasn't in the mood to talk about such things. He tasted the cognac and looked at how Sara's dark hair glistened in the lamplight. And a great longing came over him to stroke it and feel it with his cheek.

'The pipes and hoses were collected in Texas,' Howard continued, 'where this kind of equipment has been used in oil drilling, but then it turned out that curved joints weren't available. That slowed things up until a factory in Pittsburgh undertook to make these curved joints especially for us – and then everything was sent by cargo planes. By ship it would have taken much too long and could have been too late, if it is going to be of some use here, which I sincerely hope. . . .'

He was silent and looked out the window, but the eruption was at this time less than it had ever been.

'If the fish-processing and freezing plants are covered by lava, then with them would be lost one of the most fully developed fish-processing operations existing anywhere in the world today. It meets the strictest requirements of the American market—all the work rooms newly tiled, with vinyl wallpaper on the columns and so forth. Those rooms are more like a ballroom in Hotel Saga than a fish-processing plant.'

'Have they found a new transformer station?' asked Andri, trying to force himself to follow what Howard was talking about and shake off the power of the dark hair so near him.

'Yes, we are expecting a five hundred kilowatt power station with *Herjolfur*.'

'And when will a person be able to take a proper shower?' Andri asked.

'They are beginning to pump water from the old well into the system. It is probably a little salty, but fine to take a bath in. It is apparent that we could have saved more than a hundred buildings if we had had powerful enough pumping equipment,' Howard said.

At the same moment the telephone rang. Howard went into the office.

There was silence again. Andri stole a glance at Sara.

Finally she said, 'Were you all that time with your mother?'

'I was stranded in Reykjavik by the weather.'

'Was it so bad?'

'The planes weren't flying.'

'And how was your mother doing?'

'Well. She had two boxes of candy on the bedside table at Vifilstadir.' Andri smiled.

'Had she found two boyfriends then?'

'Mama doesn't let herself get bored.'

Sara chortled. She took a cigarette from the pack on the table.

'Kalli came here one night,' she said and brought the flame up to the cigarette.

'Yes, I heard that.'

'He told us a lot about some people he had known in West Germany, some of them in the Bader-Meinhoff group.'

'Not everything that Kalli says is holy writ.'

'It's all the same to me if it's not holy.' Sara leaned back and inhaled a deep drag of smoke.

'He lives in somewhat confused ideas.'

'Who doesn't?'

'Well, that's true, probably all of us have more or less confused ideas.'

They heard Howard talking into the telephone with intensity.

'They can't be anything but confused.'

She stretched out her hand to him and touched him with her finger tips. He felt lightning move all around him.

She rose up in the seat and started the record again.

A Beatle sang in a melancholy voice, 'You've got to hide your love away . . . .'

She sat up in his embrace and her fingertips touched his groin so that he jerked involuntarily like a shy horse.

What difference did it make if she was his half-sister?

They could hear Howard talking very upset on the telephone.

'And why in hell haven't they got a faster ship than *Sudri*, with this valuable equipment, since the Americans took the trouble to send it by air all this distance, many thousands of kilometres . . . .'

'I haven't thought of anything but you the whole time,' Andri whispered in her ear as they embraced and kissed. 'I was getting to be afraid that something had happened to you.'

'Come downstairs,' she whispered and he felt her tremble in his hands as though she were shivering.

They stood up and stole out silently.

Howard was still talking about pipes and pumping equipment on the phone.

*

'Why was it that you didn't come to the door?' Andri asked when they got down to their cellar room.

'I was in a trance.'

'A trance?'

'Only a part of us is here. I am always trying to get in touch with the other parts of my self.'

'And can you in a trance?'

'Yes, I sometimes meet other parts of myself and can put them together into an entity that I understand. But when I wake up from the trance it falls out of my consciousness, and nothing is left but a nagging anxiety in my heart.'

'That is just some kind of fantasy.'

'What isn't fantasy? Isn't it fantasy that we are here making love and talking together?'

'Have you spoken about this to Howard?'

'He walks in his sleep, too.'

'Too? You both walk in your sleep?'

'We got old Ella to play blindman's buff with us. It was so funny.'

'You played blindman's buff – you and Howard and old Ella?'

'She has become a little stiff now, poor old Ella.'

153

'I can't believe that old Ella played blindman's buff.'

'She does everything I tell her to.'

'What kind of blindman's buff?'

'I sometimes got Daddy to play blindman's buff with us little girls, my classmates. It was terribly exciting. He groped his way ahead with a blindfold on his eyes and tried to grab us. I remember how excited we got. . . .'

All at once the sun began to shine in the window where they were.

'We must go swim in the sea,' whispered Sara. 'It is lukewarm in the harbour from the embers. Some boys who were swimming there the other day told me.'

They dressed quickly and stole out. The sun shone on the mirror-smooth expanse of the sea. No fires were visible in the lava, only large steam clouds rising high up out of the black lava, almost motionless against the blue sky.

They went down into the town. It was very quiet except for the cry of a black guillemot which was making itself at home on its old nesting site.

Some men had pumps at the freezing plant and were looking at a black mass of lava between the buildings.

They got to the edge of the harbour without anyone appearing to notice them, over the harbour wall and onto new lava on the other side, where a black beach had taken shape, of fine sand and large lava boulders, which the sea had immediately begun to grind and polish.

The crying of the birds increased where the rocks were close on the other side of the harbour entrance, a reminder that mating time was at hand and a great competition for a convenient place in a hole or cliff ledge.

In a small nook in a large cliff they took off their clothes and waded down the steeply sloping beach, clean and free of seaweed. The sea was tepid but the morning air was cool. They swam several strokes in the vicinity of teeming eider ducks.

When they came out they let the sun dry them though there was little warmth in its rays. They ran to get warm on the barren pumice beach.

The first human footprints on the newly created earth.

III

Solveig looked around her in the hotel room. There were open suitcases and various things she had bought for the trip, though she counted of course on buying a fair amount when they came back. But it was best not to spend the first days of the honeymoon in the shops.

To think that this day had arrived in her life, so bright and fair. She cast her eyes out at the blue sky over the roofs of the houses.

The long awaited day had finally arrived.

Ahead was the wedding night itself and then the flight south into the sun, where Venice awaited them with its canals and gondolas, ancient bridges and the Piazza san Marco, full of white pigeons. There lay the tickets and the travel brochures with the enchanting pictures: a gondola with cushions and scarlet cloth glides over the mirror-smooth water in the green shadow of an antique wall with a drooping bunch of violet lilacs.

There was no atmosphere of remoteness about it, but a scene of many incidents, briefly described in the brochure, and there were names that she recognized—Romeo and Juliet.

Hannes had made some kind of joke about them. He was always so waggish now.

There lay the light summer dress that she had had made for her, since summer dresses had not come into the shops yet, and a pocketbook, gloves and shoes that went with it. They also went well with the light green suit she had bought some days ago, which fitted her perfectly. She was so lucky to take a size that there was a large selection of.

She looked at herself in the large bathroom mirror in the light dress and light shoes and was satisfied.

Yes, they had attracted the attention of the guests when they went down to get lunch today. Hannes, this elegant man of the world, not a single grey hair in his head, and she herself, fair and smelling of Chanel Number Five. She was a striking woman, there was no denying it, perhaps in some ways finer now than when she had been young, more at home in the world and more sophisticated.

Was her eye shadow a bit too dark? No, it only made her a little more mysterious, with a greater power of enchantment. And her hair was quite special, a little daring of course, but why not? Her upswept blond hair was just like a bird's nest, that was the idea of the girl in the salon, who had studied in Paris. And everyone in the salon adored this fashion. Yes, it was no wonder that the men had just about twisted their necks out of joint when Hannes and she went down to breakfast and the waiter showed them the way, with bowing and southern courtesy.

Hannes had called him Pedro and told her he came from Italy. Now they were almost half way there.

No, there weren't any wrinkles in her face after the facial, and she had slept well despite the anticipation, although it had not been entirely according to Hoyle to sleep together the night before – and also about the reception – that there wouldn't be one. Hannes had his way about that because he was so much against it. 'Just the two of us,' he had pleaded with her until she had given in, although it wasn't what she wanted. But those words, "just the two of us," had their influence and showed better than anything else how much he doted on her. Yes, this mature man of the world had almost turned into a boy for love of her. . . .

There was a knock on the door.

Could Hannes have come back so soon? So obsessively eager to be at her side.

But Hannes didn't come in, and she opened the door.

Who was this woman there before her, freckled and pale?

'Don't you still know me?' the woman asked hesitantly.

'Of course, Marsibil!—what's wrong with me?'

'Isn't my brother Hanni. . . ?'

'Come in, dear.'

Solveig almost pulled her prospective sister-in-law into the room and slammed the door shut.

'Don't call me Marsibil – everyone calls me Massa.'

'Certainly, dear, I will too. This place is full of junk, we've been buying this and that for our trip.'

'When are you going?'

'Tomorrow morning.'

Solveig picked a package up from the blue easy chair and indicated it to her prospective sister-in-law.

'Sit down Massa dear.'

'Is Hanni. . . ?'

'He went to the telephone office because of some Japanese ship, but he will be right back.'

Massa had perched on the edge of the chair.

'I need to have a word with him.'

'Yes, it's nice of you to look in on us. Unfortunately there's not going to be a reception, although I wanted one.'

'Where are you going?'

'To Venice.'

'Venice is wonderful.'

Massa rubbed her palms together. Her hands were rough and large for such a thin woman. And how plainly she was dressed, in old walking shoes.

'I barely had a chance to see you there the other day,' Massa said, and smiled in embarrassment out of one corner of her mouth.

'Then you shall do that now,' said Solveig and ran her hands down her hips. She had just had her skirt let out, but she knew that men had always given her curving hips much attention.

'And you have such fair hair.'

'I've just had it lightened. It was reddish when I was young.'

'How well you and Hanni go together, he so dark and you so fair.'

'Thank you Massa dear. Have a piece of candy. Hannes brought them yesterday. I mustn't eat them all because I have to watch my figure, although Hannes wants me a little chubby.' She handed Massa the opened candy box with a red silk ribbon.

'It's Swiss with nuts.'

'No thanks, I don't think so now,' Massa excused herself, smiling with a down-turned mouth.

'Listen, let's go downstairs and get some coffee. I didn't get a proper chance to have any a little while ago—Hannes was in such a hurry to get to the telephone office.'

'I don't know.'

'Oh yes, it's a very good idea. We can talk better there, in here I can't get my mind off these packages.'

'Is he buying a Japanese ship?'

'Probably not at the moment. At least that's not what we're taking to Venice.'

Solveig laughed, it was really witty of her. That's how happiness makes a person, funny and playful.

Solveig took several pieces out of the box, wrapped them in a paper napkin and stuck them in her purse.

'This Swiss chocolate goes so wonderfully with coffee.'

They walked along the carpeted hallway and into the elevator. There was more style in taking the elevator than walking down the stairs, even though they were only on the third floor.

She left the key at the desk and asked them to give Hannes the message that they were in the dining room having coffee.

In the dining room there were only a few people after lunch. They decided to sit on a sofa at the big window with heavy old-fashioned curtains.

There was always an air of dignity about this hotel in the centre of town, and she still remembered how impressed she had been to come here the first time, young and full of curiosity about the kind of life that took place here and that poems were written about.

Pedro greeted them with a southern gesture of the arm and seated them at the table. Solveig felt his hot glance move over her fully developed form when they took their seats. These Italians! She gave him a radiant, smiling glance in return.

'What shall it be for my ladies?' he asked.

How lightly the accent fell on the ear.

'Pedro, your coffee was so good a little while ago. . . .'

'I am happy, I am happy,' said Pedro ingratiatingly and gazed at the light green pieces of turquoise in her earrings as though he would devour them. She also had a necklace and ring with the same kind of stones.

'Coffee for both of us,' she said.

Pedro turned away lithely, his coat tails dangling behind him like the tail of a show cock.

'You know how to be pampered,' Massa said.

'I'm learning from Hannes. It's wonderful going out to eat with him, and when he chooses the wine, he takes his time and questions the waiters back and forth, really interrogates them.'

Massa tittered faintly.

She wasn't wearing any rings and had probably never been engaged. Yes, Hannes greatly excelled his brothers and sisters. Even the member of parliament had been half boorish, in scuffed shoes and dirty shirt, as though he had slept in it, when they drank coffee with him in the Circle at the Parliament building.

'I ran across some of the workmen in my father's shop,' Massa finally got around to saying. 'And when I asked them, they said they were there for my brother Hannes.'

'Yes, that's right. Everything's being changed and

160

remodelled, didn't you know that?'

'No, to tell the truth, I did not. Nor did any of us brothers and sisters.'

'And you live now over the shop.'

'That's it exactly. We think it's by far the best idea to sell the building.'

'Sell it?'

'It's got so old and dilapidated, the pipes all more or less broken, the windows rotten, and the roof useless.'

'But it's such a good location, just off Laugavegur.'

'But there's next to no lot there – and we are so many brothers and sisters.'

The waiter had come with their coffee on a tray.

They were silent as he set the cups in front of them and poured the steaming coffee into them.

'Will there be something else for my ladies?'

'No thanks, not for the moment, Pedro.'

Solveig took care not to smile too much this time. She had to be careful when they got to Italy not to be too warm in her expression. They could misunderstand it, these hot-blooded southerners.

Massa did not use sugar in her coffee. She herself took one piece.

'Hannes has told me that you are his favourite sister. There has always been a special closeness between the two of you that the others do not share'.

A faint blush came to Massa's pale cheeks and she said a bit secretively, 'Yes, there has always been a special relationship between my brother Hannes and me, and yet. . . .'

'Here is the candy to have with our coffee,' said Solveig and spread out the napkin with the pieces on the table in front of them.

'Have one.' She took one herself.

Massa took the smallest piece and began to nibble on it.

161

'But he cannot have my father's workshop and store changed without consulting us.'

'He's had so much to do since we came from the sanitarium,' Solveig said in his defence.

'But he didn't say a word about it the other day when he came to see me,' Massa complained.

'At home?'

'No, in Paradise. He often comes there and gets the special of the day when he is in a hurry.'

'What are you saying—Paradise?'

'Yes, the vegetarian restaurant where I work. Hasn't Hanni ever told you about it?'

'No, we talk mostly about the future, because that is what we will share from now on.'

'God willing.'

'I hope you are not. . . .'

'No, no, it's just an expression I use. I am so superstitious, pay no attention to it.'

'Yes, God willing. There's no harm in saying that. If you work in Paradise then you are in a damn good place. In paradise itself.'

'Oh, I don't know about that,' Massa said somewhat miserably. 'Only vegetarians come there, and some of the old geezers are terribly eccentric and critical. One of them told me the other day that he hadn't been able to sleep because his neighbour had a dog.'

'That barked at night?'

'No, no.'

'Then why?'

'Because the dog had shit on the pavement.'

They both laughed, and immediately it was as if they had grown closer.

They sipped their coffee.

Most of the guests had left the dining room, and they heard

the waiters back in the kitchen talking together and the sound of women laughing in the intervals.

'It would be best if you spoke to Hannes about it yourself,' Solveig said. 'But I trust that you won't oppose our having the space. We have really been counting on it.'

'No, I wouldn't do anything,' said Massa and tried to smile at her prospective sister-in-law. 'My brother Hanni is used to getting his own way.'

They heard the cathedral bells ring softly, probably announcing the end of a funeral.

'Tell me in complete confidence, just between the two of us, Massa, because Hannes and I talk only about the future, has he ever owned a car?'

'No, he has never needed to. He has lived with Abigail and always had her car.'

'What kind of car was it?'

'A big American car. She got herself a new car every other year and they drove our mother to Fljotshlid.'

'Did he live with her all the time?'

'Yes, most of the time—except that he stayed sometimes with our mother.'

'Why was that?'

'Oh I don't know, but Abba was always terribly nice to Mother and invited her to go on car trips with them.'

'Do you know why it was that Hannes left her?'

'No, I don't know, but the week before he went into the National Hospital for tests he was home with us, and Mother went into the old people's home because her memory was so bad, always forgetting the coffee pot on the hot plate, and twice it set the house on fire. Hannes was home then, just before Christmas, and could put the fire out right away, but the house could just as easily have gone up in flames in a moment. It singed his eyebrows.'

'I'm really not interested in knowing anything about this

163

Abigail, she has nothing to do with me,' said Solveig coldly.

'Won't you join me in another piece of candy?' she asked Massa.

'No thanks, but I would not mind a glass of water.'

'Are you feeling ill?'

'No, I always have to be careful of my stomach.'

Solveig hit her cup with a teaspoon and Pedro immediately appeared and strode toward them.

'More freshly brewed coffee?' he asked. 'First-class-prima.'

'No thank you. Just a glass of water for the lady.'

Pedro vanished again.

At that moment Hannes appeared at the double door and did not take long in spotting them on the sofa.

'There you are my doves.' He bent down to his fiancée and kissed her lightly on the cheek.

'Forgive me, darling, for making you wait, but these conversations with the Japanese can take up some time—and Massa, it's good to see you.'

He kissed her too on the pale cheek.

'Yes, she has been so sweet to keep me company the whole time,' Solveig said and smiled her most affectionate smile at Massa.

Hannes took a seat with them and signalled the waiter to bring him a cup and saucer.

'I was apologizing to her for not having a wedding reception and inviting the relatives.'

'Romeo and Juliet didn't have a wedding reception,' said Hannes and smiled so broadly that the creases in his cheeks turned into deep incisions and the silver fillings were visible in his yellow molars.

The waiter came with the cup and saucer for Hannes and a glass of water for his sister Massa.

'How is your colon, Massa?' he asked when the waiter had left the table.

'Not so good,' answered Massa, who had slipped a pill into her mouth and then drank from the glass of water.

'It's extraordinary not to be cured by the food in the vegetarian restaurant, which ought to be so wholesome,' Solveig said.

'No, the people in Paradise all have acid indigestion,' answered Hannes and laughed.

'Maybe that's what was wrong with Adam,' he added and laughed again at his wit, and Solveig with him, but his sister Massa was not amused.

'It proves as it did before, Massa,' her brother said and stood up from the table, 'that even in Paradise itself life can go sour.'

'Should we go?' asked Solveig.

'Yes, time is passing.'

He looked at his gold wrist watch, doubtless a gift from this Abigail thought Solveig with a pang in her heart.

Solveig wrapped the last piece of candy in the white napkin and put it into her purse.

'Are we going now to the old people's home to see your mother?' she asked.

'Yes, we are. Where are you going, Massa? Shouldn't I run you home?'

'No thanks, I need to go to the flower shop and buy Easter lilies. I always put Easter lilies on Daddy's grave on his birthday.'

'You're right, it's today.'

'No, tomorrow, have you forgotten it?'

'I always rely on you to remember it, Massa dear.'

He led his fiancée forward and motioned to Pedro with his fingers.

'Yes, you are safe doing that,' said Massa on the way out with them. 'It is a day I will never forget, Daddy's birthday.'

*

On the way in the taxi Solveig told her fiancé about the

conversation with Massa, and her reaction to the alterations they had planned for his mother's house.

'Don't worry about it. There have always been nothing but lions in the path of my sister Massa, and yet she has never got so much as a scratch.'

Solveig slipped her hand into his.

'What hair tonic did you have the barber put on you this morning?' she whispered.

'It's Soir de Paris. I've used it before sometimes.'

'Did Abigail like it?'

'No, she couldn't stand it.'

'Then you must go on using it. I think it suits you so well.'

He squeezed her hand in consent as the taxi stopped outside the old people's home.

'Did you buy the Japanese ship?'

'You don't just buy a ship like you do a book, not even a rare book like a Gudbrand's Bible,' he answered, taking her by the arm when he had paid the taxi.

'No, I was just wondering about it.'

When they came into the hallway of the old people's home elderly people were moving about aimlessly. Two old women sat on a bench holding hands, like children in a place where they felt insecure.

They were met by an odour that was like a blend of wax and rotten sauerkraut. Solveig tried not to breathe deeply.

The floors were gleaming and the walls smelled of green soap.

'I forgot to bring anything for your mother,' she whispered to her fiancé.

'That doesn't matter, she doesn't like anything except licorice, pharmaceutical licorice.'

But the old woman was not in her room. They found her in the sitting room at the other end of the hall.

It was a carpeted room with easy chairs and small tables.

Hannes was quick to spot his mother, went over to her and greeted her affectionately. But she was not impressed.

'Mama, aren't you happy to see me?' he asked, and gave her a filial kiss on a cheek darkened with age.

'What are you doing here?' she answered grumpily.

'Mama, this is a woman I want to introduce you to. Her name is Solveig and we are going to get married today.'

'What does that have to do with me?' she said and picked up a handkerchief to wipe her nose. It was a big nose like Hannes's, evidence of their kinship, and it nearly reached her thin hairy chin.

'We can sit here,' said Solveig, indicating a small sofa with a table next to it.

Hannes led his mother over to the couch, where she and Solveig sat down, and he brought a straight chair for himself.

Solveig tried to act tenderly and whispered, 'Call me Solla, everyone calls me Solla.'

The old woman looked at her necklace with the green stones.

'Be careful of that,' she said, 'otherwise he will steal it from you.'

'What silliness, Mama, you know I have never stolen anything from you.'

'Oh yes, you and the others want to steal everything I own, and that's why I'm here.'

'I'm not the one who was responsible. It was Massa and the others. And you know you can always be with me, Mama, if you are in any trouble.'

Solveig could not bring herself to tell the old woman that she would be welcome to stay with them, so she remained silent.

'And how are the heart valves?' asked the old woman, finally looking at her son.

'Don't worry about that.'

'I thought your brother could get Parliament to pay your bills. They don't have anything better to do with their money.'

167

'Something will work out,' her son answered brusquely.

'Here, I've brought you a little something,' said Solveig, who had taken the piece of candy out of the napkin from her purse.

She put the piece of candy in the old woman's mouth. Her cheeks were deeply sunken.

'Why don't you have your teeth in, Mama?' her son asked.

'Stjana stole them from me, but that doesn't matter because they hurt me anyway.'

'Then you should see the dentist here, he must come now and then. . . .'

But the old woman wasn't listening to him. She had begun to spit and retch. She let the chocolate drip down into her palm and tried to dry it with the same cloth she had used before to blow her nose with.

'What kind of outlandish filth is this?' she muttered.

'It's the finest Swiss chocolate,' said her prospective daughter-in-law. 'Hannes brought me a box of it yesterday.'

'Yes, it was the most expensive kind,' Hannes confirmed.

His mother kept on spitting. Tracks ran down from the corners of her mouth and the cloth was soaked with chocolate mush. An old woman who had been mumbling to herself in the centre of the floor came over to them with her hand stretched out—'Give me.'

'I am sorry, but we don't have anything,' said Hannes and looked at the woman with an expression almost of terror.

But his mother gave the woman the cloth, and she ran away with it, sucking on it continually.

Solveig groaned, 'Oh my God.'

'That wasn't candy,' said the old woman, 'it was dog shit.'

'What silliness, Mama, we don't want to give you anything but the best.'

'Here is my handkerchief,' said the prospective daughter-in-law, who had taken a small handkerchief out of her purse smelling of Chanel Number Five. She dried her hands with it.

The nurse came in and looked around the room. Everything was in perfect order, with the old people furtively scrutinizing the guests.

'Mama,' Hannes said ceremoniously, 'I have a little document here for you to sign.'

'So you can sell the house,' snapped the old woman.

'No, no—not at all,' her son assured her. 'So you can perhaps come back to it when it is finished being fixed up, with double-pane glass and things like that.'

'And who is going to pay for that?'

'I will see to that Mama, don't worry about it.'

'But haven't we always had to worry about you, didn't your father have to let all the gold. . . ?'

'There, there, Mama,' said Hannes soothingly, 'you've got everything a little mixed up.'

'Well, if Abba agrees then it ought to be all right. Do you want to do it, Abba dear?'

They pretended not to notice her slip of the tongue. Hannes had taken the folded yellow document out of his inside pocket and spread it out on the small table in front of the old woman.

'Here's where you write your name on this,' he said, pointing to the document with a type-written text.

'And who will pay for the windows?' the old woman asked.

'Don't be concerned about that—we will see to it.' He handed his mother his fountain pen, large and black.

'Aren't you going to help your mother write her name?' asked Solveig.

'There's no need to—she's able to do it herself.'

The old woman grasped the writing implement with a sneer, and in an instant she had signed her name to the document. The letters were firmly and clearly formed.

'Now you can get married,' she said with a sarcastic expression on her face.

169

'But your handwriting is so beautiful,' said the prospective daughter-in-law while she surreptitiously ran her eye over the text of the document. But she didn't have her reading glasses and could not make it out very well.

'You won't be seeing us again until after the honeymoon,' said her son and put his arms tightly around her shoulders. He folded the document and put it in his inside pocket.

'And where are you going?' asked the old woman, beginning to rock back and forth on the sofa.

'We're taking a honeymoon in Venice,' said Solveig and looked tenderly at her prospective mother-in-law.

'And naturally you will expect to pay for the whole thing, Abba dear, as you have always done before.'

'Mama, when will you get it into your head that this is not Abba, it is Solveig, from Westman Islands.'

'Although really from the East,' added Solveig.

'And you want to go there on your honeymoon?' asked the old woman, looking at each of them in turn with distant, water-blue eyes.

'Yes, to Venice in Italy,' answered her prospective daughter-in-law.

'And how will you get to land, isn't there a terrible surf there?'

'We'll travel by air,' her son answered curtly.

'One time a man I knew drowned there getting to land,' the old woman continued, as though she was beginning a long tale of hardship.

'But this is Venice, not Westman Islands,' her son said with annoyance.

'You know, where the gondolas are and the canals,' whispered her prospective daughter-in-law gently.

'He was going in toward land in some kind of gondola,' the old woman continued with her story, 'and landed in the surf. It was horrible. The blessed man couldn't swim and what happened happened. Do you both know how to swim?'

'Yes, of course we know how to swim,' said her son, shifting his weight impatiently from one foot to the other. 'But right now we aren't able to spend any longer with you, we have so many things to take care of.'

'Yes, we could just look in briefly this time,' said the fiancée and stood up from the sofa next to the old woman.

'But you have grown so short, Abba dear,' said the old woman looking her over. 'Have you shrunk?'

'Mama, do I still have to tell you that this is not Abigail, this is Solveig, called Solla. Do try now to remember that.'

'Don't think, Hanni, that I will permit you or any of the rest of you to talk to me like some kind of helpless fool, even though you have put me in this place against my will,' said his mother angrily.

She stretched herself and held her nose high, obviously an old family inheritance from past centuries that she was proud to own.

'Oh, no, Mama, I didn't mean it that way,' her son hastened to assure her.

'He is so fond of you,' whispered Solveig in the old woman's ear.

'Fond of me,' the old woman snorted, 'he has never been fond of anything, and you better learn how to swim before you go out in a gondola with him. A word to the wise.'

'Let's go,' Hannes said quickly to his fiancée and took her arm, 'this isn't getting anywhere.'

The nurse came to the door and announced loudly that visiting hours were over.

'How beautiful the tulips are in the vase,' said Hannes charmingly to the nurse in the doorway.

'We do our best to make things as pleasant for the old people as we can,' said the nurse, looking the room over, 'but sometimes it's difficult to manage.'

171

'Kristjan ate four tulips this morning,' the old woman said as they went out into the hallway. 'He was lucky they weren't roses.'

'We'll stay longer next time,' Solveig whispered to the old woman out by the stairs. 'We'll have more time then.'

'I know you will drive me sometime in your car,' said the old woman sniffing. 'I'll try not to get car sick like I did last time.'

The prospective daughter-in-law kissed the old woman lightly on the cheek in parting and the son also gave her a gentle caress, but she paid scant attention to it.

When they got down to the entrance door they waved goodbye to her where she stood at the top of the stairs, lifting her bony hands as if in prayer.

'My God, I am glad that's over,' Solveig sighed as her fiancé took her arm and led her out into the cool sunshine and along the flower beds, where long rows of tulips stretched their heads up to meet the cold, bright spring air.

*

They had come to the office of the clerk of the City court to be registered as a married couple. Hannes knew the man personally.

They signed the contract in the presence of the clerk, with the office typist as a witness, as well as a man who was there on other business.

Solveig detected the odour of sweat from under the girl's arm when she signed her name, and she noticed too how the man's thumbs curled back.

'Why am I putting up with this?' she said to herself while they read through the form.

The clerk dug with his thumb up in his nose.

'Why didn't I get married in the cathedral, as I always dreamed of?'

But it was too late now. Afterwards Solveig remembered better the cooing of the pigeons outside the window than what had happened in the clerk's office.

Most likely her senses and natural responses had been numbed by trudging up all those worn stairs to the fourth floor of the grey concrete building by the Lake.

They heard the cathedral bell strike, so close were they to the place where she had seen herself before the altar on a red plush carpet, the dark blue starry ceiling arching over her, and the bridegroom putting a gold ring on her finger and kissing her in candle light, and the benediction of the priest in his ceremonial collar and all the devout faces shining on them from the congregation on this festive occasion that was hers alone, and which she was now deprived of.

It wasn't until she had come out into the open air that she asked herself what had been written in the small print of the contract, something about an apartment which Hannes had the right to take if they separated. . . ?

But it was too late now to think of that, and also no danger of their marriage going bad, where there were no young children to get on their nerves.

Hannes took her firmly by the hand. There Austurvollur Square came into view, almost green again, except where ice had lain during the winter and left brown patches of frost damage. Thin branches on the shrubs had begun to swell.

'Why doesn't Hannes own a car?' she asked herself. Massa had said that he always had this Abigail's car, this rich woman he had lived with. 'Why hasn't he mentioned her until finally at the end?'

And why in the world were these questions coming to her, when she ought to rejoice and be happy on this bright sunny day?

They walked hand-in-hand across Austurvollur. A young man in jeans, with a downy beard, turned to them and held pins up in front of them that he was selling.

'Do you want to buy a Vietnam pin?' he asked, 'a memento of Nixon and Pompidou coming here?'

The pin had the dark blue and orange colours of the Vietnam flag with the words Peace and Freedom in Vietnam.

'No thank you,' said Solveig, 'We don't buy pins like that.'

The young man smirked, but some sailors who were sitting on a bench with a bottle called to him.

The newlyweds walked on. The cries of the newspaper boys came to them and the murmur of traffic at rush hour, just before the stores closed.

'Should we go up to the hotel right away?' Solveig asked.

'No, we should get to the travel agency before it closes to find out if there have been any changes in the flight on account of the air traffic controllers' strike in Britain,' Hannes said.

'Oh, I hope not. I am longing so to get to Italy.'

They went down to Austurstræti where there was a swarming crowd of people, everyone in a hurry.

They received confirmation at the travel agency that there would be no change in the schedule because it was a non-stop flight to Italy.

They walked back to Posthusstræti on the way to the hotel.

Hotel Borg had been a place that Solla always thought gave off a special brilliance when she first came to the capital, and it particularly pleased her to be able to spend her wedding night there, if only they had been married in the cathedral instead of that shabby office. And there would be no reception, such as she had so often imagined, with speeches and toasts.

She had only met Hannes's brother in the entrance of the Parliament building. He had been too busy with committee work to be able to spend a few minutes with them. There was perhaps a chance that they could expect Nixon and Pompidou to come onto the floor of the world's oldest parliament and greet the members. He could have invited them to a glass of champagne

174

in the Circle.

Why couldn't she stop thinking about all this, when the weather was so fine on this auspicious day of their marriage.

Later they were going to get an apéritif before the dinner that Hannes had ordered. It was a menu he had spent a long time composing, and was based on his experience over the whole world in the course of buying and selling ships.

They had reached the entrance of the hotel when someone called out behind them.

'Hannes, Hannes.'

They stopped on the pavement.

A smiling man came up to them with his hand in the air.

'Where have you caught that fairy princess?' the man asked.

'We are coming back from getting married,' said Hannes.

'May I wish you happiness,' he said and put his arms around them both.

'Slender fairy princess,' he said exhaling a bitter breath in Solveig's face.

'But unfortunately I have nothing to give you except my best wishes.'

'That's all right,' said Hannes, wanting to get out of the man's embrace.

'But listen, old friend, all the banks are closed, are you able to. . . ?'

'No, I'm sorry,' answered Hannes and tried to shove the man away from them. He still held Hannes by the hand.

'What is the meaning of this?' said Hannes harshly.

'You know exactly what it means, old fox,' the man said, and had stopped smiling.

'Hannes, who is this man?' Solveig wailed.

'Tell her who I am.'

With a quick jerk Hannes broke away from the man, who shouted something after them about a fat fairy princess as they hurried into the hotel, where a ribbon-bedecked young attendant

175

opened the door for them.

'What man was that really?' Solveig said when they came into the hotel lobby.

'I should have been on my guard against him.'

Hannes was out of breath from the struggle out on the pavement, and he was still puffing in the elevator on the way up to their floor.

There was still plenty of time before they could go down to get their apéritif.

Solveig went over to the window while her husband went into the bathroom to wash his hands after the scuffle.

She looked at white clouds sailing quickly in the blue sky above the Parliament building. This day of destiny had not begun too well: first came Hannes's sister Massa, then the visit to the old people's home, and finally this bird of ill omen.

What did it portend for her?

Had she acted too quickly? Had she been too eager to have this long-awaited dream come true?

No, she tried to push those doubts aside. But from the bathroom the groom was heard rinsing his mouth with loud gargling sounds.

IV

Howard was in his office at home when he saw *Sudri* come sailing into the harbour. Finally the ship had arrived with the long-awaited cargo that people had quarrelled so much about, and that had been sent by transport planes all the way from America. On the wharf, the professor who invented seawater cooling was at the front of the crowd. Until now he had had to use small pipes and weak pumps, but with this powerful equipment he expected to be able to prove the effectiveness of seawater cooling against a lava flow.

As soon as *Sudri* had docked, work was begun unloading all the large equipment.

'When these pipes are working,' the professor said, 'they should be able to pump over a thousand litres of sea water a second.'

'I never heard the sea measured in litres before,' said one of the longshoremen.

'That's about like a medium-sized river,' the professor explained.

'It won't do any more good against a lava flow than pissing on a house fire,' said another one of them looking toward the professor playfully.

'That all depends on how big you are,' the professor answered.

'I am sure we could have saved many buildings in this last surge if this equipment had been working,' said Howard.

Engineers explained where the pipes should be laid and how the pumping system should work. Four lines with twelve-inch

177

steel pipe were laid from the sea up to the lava. One line came out of a barge west of the southern wall of the harbour, and the others came from inside the harbour. The water was pumped out of the sea with seven low-pressure pumps. They were then joined by thirty high-pressure pumps, which lifted the water up to the lava, sixty metres above sea-level. From the pumps ran about five kilometres of eight-inch plastic pipe, which was made in Iceland and had proved to be very good. It would bend if there were motion on the lava and not break. It was also easy to take apart if necessary, to move back in case of a new surge.

A crew of men was appointed to lay a new road into the hot and rough-surfaced lava.

Because of the heat and clouds of steam, the practice was adopted of driving in stakes and stringing lines between them so that people could feel their way along them when they could not open their eyes in the steam. One after another the men with the hoses had to take off their boots because of the heat and cool their soles with streams of seawater.

The geologists came up and showed them how the seawater cooling could change streams of molten lava into reliable protective walls. The lava could not slide straight down in front of the whole tephra mass but instead had to lift itself over its own crust, and therefore rather than running off at the lowest point of the wall it had to go over the top of it.

Of greatest importance was getting the lines in as far as possible onto the standing lava so that the sea water could sink down through it to where the molten lava underneath was still 1100 degrees and cool it. The lava production at the crater was still about fifty tons a second, but the main weight of it ran toward the sea, in the opposite direction from the harbour, as it had since the beginning.

In a slight surge that took place the first night after *Sudri* came with the equipment, several tons of lava pressed over the wharf and ran into the harbour. That was the first lava that had got all the way down, and people were afraid that it might not be long before the harbour was filled and the structures on the wharf crushed under the weight of lava. The edge of the lava had come right up to the freezing plant and had broken the corner of one building on the second floor and filled two rooms with tephra.

Every possible effort was made to get the new pipes working, but the surge subsided without doing more damage.

It was obvious to people that there was a good chance all the equipment in the freezing plant would go the same way as the transformer in the power plant. This was the last chance to pull it out of the buildings and get it on board ship before it was too late. On the other hand, that would mean a great delay in restoring commercial life when the eruption was over.

Andri was with his crew up on the slope next to the main crater, where it was necessary to pump sea water to an elevation of sixty metres. It was a sunny day. Journalists with movie cameras were taking pictures of all the equipment and the geologists with their meters and scientific instruments. A green colour was beginning to spread out into the loose gravel of the black mountain sides and the rock cliffs, and the puffins had started moving into their houses. Soon they would be scratching out their holes, like the people who were hard at work sweeping the roofs of houses and cleaning streets of pumice and dust.

Howard had come out onto the lava to observe the birds' preparations. He had his binoculars and pointed them toward the birds he was watching. Migratory birds had started to arrive from over the ocean to the south, and they sometimes rested in large flocks on the Islands, having flown many hundreds of kilometres over the open sea, where there were no islands to rest on.

Andri saw a raven heading out to Bjarnarey, where he would have his nest on a cliff ledge. And he thought of the shearing trips he had been able to take as a child, going with the men out to the island, where they kept sheep until slaughtering time.

The kids were allowed to help with shearing the sheep and got to roll the wool sacks down the high grassy hillside, where the boat lay by the low flat rocks below. There men caught the wool sacks when they came rolling down the grassy slope and put them into the stern of the boat. Andri recalled how little the boat seemed to him down below and how big the sea, appearing to stretch out to infinity.

Not long ago, such a reminiscence would have been appropriate material for the poet. But other criteria were now in effect, and Andri rejected any words that might come into his mind in a romantic worship of nature.

From nearby he heard Kalli talking about the meeting that was planned between President Pompidou of France and President Nixon of the United States in Reykjavik within a few weeks.

'What could they be going to do here?' asked one of the firemen.

'Don't you know that the Eskimos leave old people they want to get rid of out on skerries to die?' answered Kalli.

'But these aren't old people,' came from another man.

'They are both finished. Tricky Dick is trying to gnaw his tail off to slip out of the Watergate trap that he caught himself in—and Pompidou is all swollen with dropsy and will soon be dead.'

'Could there be some reason for them to meet here in the middle of the Atlantic Ocean?' asked Andri.

'They're just meeting at a mid-point, like old heroes duelling on an island,' proposed another one of the firemen.

'It's your job as a poet, Andri, to reveal where the secret plots are laid,' said Kalli, and then added in a lower voice, as if in confidence, 'although I really believe that weather-Grimur will out-fox you because he has such a wide field of vision from the lighthouse on Storhofdi and knows what direction the wind blows from.'

*

Later in the day Andri noticed Howard still out bird watching, but who was that with him? Andri stopped. They were a
long way off and didn't seem to be aware of him. Yes, there
was no doubt but that it was Sara with him. Howard had his
binoculars and handed them to her. She put them up to her eyes
and looked out at the ocean. Howard pointed something out to
her, maybe some birds they were watching—or islands or
skerries?

Andri squatted down so as not to be prominent in the landscape if she looked through the binoculars in his direction, but
she didn't. She leaned on Howard, that was not disguised.

Yes, she plainly pressed herself up against him.

It came to Andri as a painful shock. Many nights they had
spent together, at her place in the cellar or at his place in the
shop, although for some reason she liked that much less.

Could she at the same time have had an intimate relationship
with Howard? And that was the reason she would rather be in
the house?

No, he rejected such suspicions. And yet?

Why were they standing so close together?

Andri crouched down in a hollow and lay there spying for
some time before they turned and went down to the town.

He had no peace of mind for the rest of the day, and in the
evening he decided to go visit her. He would act as if nothing
were wrong and wait for her to mention the bird-watching
expedition with Howard. It would prove to him that there was
nothing special between them except good friendship and their
family relationship.

It had not grown dark yet when he went to see her. Clouds
were tinged with gold over the western horizon.

He knocked at the door. No one came, so he knocked again.

181

He heard footsteps inside, and old Ella came to the door.

'Is Sara at home?' he asked.

'No,' the old woman said, 'No.'

'Oh—has she gone out perhaps?'

'No.'

Andri looked in bewilderment at the old woman. There were long hairs on her chin.

'She has gone.'

'Gone? Where?'

'To Reykjavik.'

'To Reykjavik? When?'

'Now—now this evening.'

Old Ella looked at him with her colourless eyes as if she saw through him or he were nothing more than a spirit.

'So she went to Reykjavik—now this evening?'

Ella stared at him vacantly. She was in fact homely, with a big flat nose and eyes that almost converged into one.

And that's right: he had heard a plane taking off while they were eating dinner in the cafeteria.

Maybe that is why she had gone on the walk with Howard.

But why hadn't she told him what she was thinking about when they were together the night before? Had it come up so quickly? Her mother falling ill, or something of that sort?

'Did her mother call her?' Andri asked.

'I don't know anything about it,' Ella replied, obviously impatient to get him out of the doorway.

Howard was probably not home either, perhaps having gone with her up to the airport.

But Andri could see that nothing would be gained by asking the old woman about anything else, and said goodbye.

'Would you close the gate after you,' she called to him gruffly when he went across the pavement away from the house.

It was not like the old woman to concern herself with whether the gate was open or closed, as dilapidated as it had become, and it was not easy for Andri to fasten it, with one hinge broken off and the posts rotten.

He went home to the shop and tried to lose himself in an Agatha Christie murder mystery. But he could not concentrate on the characters or the plot.

He could not stop wondering why Sara had gone so unexpectedly to Reykjavik, when the phone rang.

It was Sara.

'Where are you,' he shouted, 'in Reykjavik?'

'No, no, that was a misunderstanding of Ella's. I told her that I was going to Reykjavik, and she took it too literally and thought I had left.'

'Are you home at the Consul's house now?'

'Yes, I came downstairs and then Ella told me about this.'

'What are you doing?'

'Talking to you on the phone.'

'I mean what were you doing?'

'I was taking a bath—I blended into the water—you know we are nothing but hydrogen and a little stardust. . . .'

She had often talked to him before about her perceptions as she lay in water, preferably letting herself float like plankton on the surface and losing all sensation except of herself as part of the water, and the water was she—and so she would rise up out of the water when the ray of life touched her. It was all very obscure talk.

'Yes, Ella thought I had gone because she had not heard anything of me, and I was in fact out in space, so very far away and yet so close. . . no, I can't describe it in ordinary language, least of all over the phone—I can only experience it.'

'I can come over,' he said, feeling as he said it that he was being too eager.

'No, no, you can't do that. I called specifically to warn you. By no means may you come over.'

'Why not? It isn't so late.'

183

'That doesn't matter. You must not come, by no means, not now, later. . . .'

'I don't understand.'

'Little wonder, I probably don't either. The brain doesn't comprehend such things, they are on another plane. But you must not come, by no means, you have to promise me that.'

He thought he heard a whisper next to her.

'Is someone with you?'

'Someone is always with us, and the one who is with you also warns you, although you don't hear it. You close yourself to it. You should try to open yourself, feel that you are not alone. You should.'

She murmured something that he did not understand.

'Is someone preventing you from coming—or me?'

He felt his heart pounding and he was hardly able to control his voice.

Could Howard be standing next to her, giving her signals, holding her close, and she in nothing but her bathrobe?

'There is so much at stake,' she whispered.

'What? What is at stake?'

She was silent and he heard her breathing in the phone. It reminded him of other nights and it aroused his desire for her.

'What's at stake? You have to tell me that, or otherwise I will come.'

'No, no, no,' she cried out again into the phone. 'You must not, you must not show yourself, by no means.'

'Show myself to whom? What do you mean?'

'Oh, I can't explain it. I'm not allowed to. All communication would be broken and I would be out of touch again. You have to be patient. You must not offend the forces. They would get even and turn against us. . . .'

'What forces are you talking about? I don't understand you.'

'You should just try to open yourself.'

'Sara, listen to me, I just want to know. . . .'

'Don't ask too many question, everything will get out of balance—but I understand deep down, oh no, I can't hold onto it. Try to get in touch in water—try to feel. . . .'

She took a deep breath, as though she were almost suffocating.

'Sara, isn't there something wrong with you?'

'No, no—did you see the clouds this evening?'

'Yes, they were beautiful. I was thinking of you exactly then.'

'Did you see me in them?'

'Maybe so' slipped out without his thinking about it.

'Oh how relieved I am. Now I am much more at ease. I feel that we are reunited. But I have to go now. Goodnight, darling, think of me in the clouds.'

He wanted to tell her where he had seen her during the day, walking with Howard, not in any cloud, but she was no longer on the line.

Afterwards he sat half-dressed on the bed and wondered whether he should not go over to her house. She must be sick, she had never talked to him like that before. But he thought surely no one would answer the door if he knocked, and he could not very well call the doctor, although he knew there was a night shift at the hospital.

He heard it starting to rain and he peered out the window, but there was nothing to see, just the coal-black surroundings, like an abandoned mine.

He lay back down and tried to calm himself, but the low tones of the volcano sounded in his ears like an invocation of the deepest forces of evil.

*

All the next day, while Andri was out on the lava working on the new road and laying pipes, his mind was on the telephone conversation the night before and the steps he should take if she

185

did not come to see him tonight or did not get in touch with him.

He did not see anything of Howard. A transport ship came into the harbour during the day and tied up at the dock to pick up equipment and machinery that had been ordered moved to Reykjavik.

An x-ray machine and other valuable instruments from the hospital waited in containers down on the wharf.

Howard had at the last moment opposed dismantling the freezing plant and sending the filleting machines and pans and other bulky pieces of equipment for storage to Reykjavik, saying that they would get rough treatment in moving and might be ruined by what happened to them in inferior storage facilities.

The rain had not gone on for long, and it was clearing again, with cold, blustery wind from the north, a high-pressure system once again over northeastern Greenland.

That evening when he finished eating in the cafeteria, he wondered whether or not to phone Sara. He decided not to, trying instead to concentrate on the television news programme, but there was no way he could hold his mind on it. He began to look around for her, as if he believed she was waiting for him somewhere outside. That was only an illusion, she was nowhere to be seen. She did not appear suddenly out of her hiding place as he had half-way expected her to.

Finally, it was too much for him to take any longer, and he decided to go out to the Consul's house and find out what he should be on guard against. He had every right to do so.

He stopped along the way and looked around, not entirely wanting to be guilty of violating her restriction. Then he saw Howard from a long way off, coming out of the Consul's house in a windbreaker, with a walking stick in his hand and a baseball cap on.

His binoculars hung in a leather case from his shoulder.

Howard greeted him in a friendly way, with no ambiguity in

his manner.

'I'm going to watch birds,' he said, 'do you want to come along?'

'I don't know,' Andri answered. 'I really came to see Sara, if she's at home.'

'Well, I think it would be better if you came a little later,' Howard said. 'She has been in bed all day. Ella was going up to see her.'

'What is wrong with her?' asked Andri, hoping that now he would get the explanation of her strange conversation the night before.

'Come along with me,' Howard invited, 'and I will try to tell you about it.'

Howard pointed toward the hollow beside the hospital.

They began walking.

'I called her last night,' Andri said when they had walked a little way. 'She spoke very strangely, I couldn't understand what she was saying at all.'

'Yes, she has been very upset these days. I've been half afraid myself about her health, but there is no breakdown or clear-cut derangement. Instead there are revelations that we are unfamiliar with, although they can be quite extraordinary—and real to those who do experience them.'

'So you believe in them?'

'Believe? I don't know whether I believe. Some of what she has told me is amazing. She has some kind of mysterious powers that are at times very hard on her, but which can also lift her to the clouds.'

'It's funny you should express it that way, because last night she said she had been "in a cloud" and thought that I had seen her.'

'In this condition she always plays on words, which people have to interpret and to answer in a similar fashion in order to free her from a kind of obsession.'

187

'Do you think she meant the eruption?'

'No, I'm not certain. That seems to be decreasing rapidly.'

'I hear the same thing from the geologists.'

They had gone up beyond the hospital. The sun was sinking in the ocean, fire-red, and the sky was full of omens. This cool bright weather from the north would probably continue, as often in the spring, with frost at night and thawing in sheltered places in the sun during the day.

'It's impossible for me to believe in any "contact with spirits," but what lives deep in the mind is impossible for anyone to know. It is entirely unexamined by science. She told me this evening that my firebirds were waiting.'

'So you spoke to her tonight?'

'She had old Ella call to me to tell me that.'

'Firebirds. How do you interpret that?'

'That's not difficult because the last few evenings I've gone out looking for birds in the lava. They are liable to be paralyzed with fear when they land on the burning hot lava, and go into a sort of shock. They are unable to fly away, but just flutter around, and can get seriously burned. I have found several birds in this shape recently, some so badly burned that they could not live, others less burned that have probably been able to survive after I have got them out.'

They walked obliquely up the ridge between the new lava and Helgafell.

Howard started talking about migratory birds, what species he had seen and what kind of weather they must have had this week coming over the ocean.

Sometimes when they got caught in bad storms over the ocean their energy would be used up and they would perish in large numbers on the way to their nesting grounds, but nothing could keep them from setting out on the difficult and dangerous journey many hundreds of miles over the open sea, along routes they established millions of years back in time, even over islands and areas of land which were now long since sunk into the ocean. Often it had happened that flocks of migratory birds suddenly perched on a ship at sea, the birds so weak from opposing storm and cold that crewmen were able to pick them up in their bare hands.

'And so we all live according to patterns that have developed over millions of years and cannot free ourselves from them with pompous resolutions or hard-hitting propaganda,' Howard said.

Andri asked whether the puffins had not begun to dig out their holes.

'Oh yes, they are cleaning up and also the petrels and the shearwaters, which I wasn't so sure would come back.'

'But the cormorants haven't come back to the harbour,' Howard added, 'since there is nothing for them to eat. The high temperature of the water has killed all the seaweed. But the seaweed will soon re-establish itself and the cormorants will be only too ready to return.'

They continued up along the ravine where the firemen had been strengthening the defences with twelve-inch steel pipes. Now and then a roar could be heard from the crater and it gushed spouts of pumice and slag.

Andri was considering how he might find an occasion to leave Howard and hurry to meet Sara, but Howard kept on talking about birds and his observations.

'What do you think about Kalli?' Andri asked in order to turn his thought in another direction.

'What I think of Kalli—well I think that in many respects he is right, but based on the wrong assumptions, and I have told him that openly. Kalli is a revolutionary because that is his method of making his way to leadership, although he will explain it in another way. It is a million-year-old pattern, all the way back to the prehistoric lizards, each of whom had its own territory. He has not surprised me, besides which I will be on my way out of here before long.'

Andri said, 'What? Haven't you liked it here? The eruption has of course changed everything.'

'No, no, it didn't change anything for me. It was nothing but romanticism to think about coming back.'

'I never considered you a romantic.'

'I mean I thought that I *could* come back, rejoin the people I had known and sometimes remembered.'

'You haven't been here long enough.'

'I had been away too long. A certain number of things are forgotten and die when a person is away for a long time, others are confused in recollection or live on in a special light—a kind of strange radiance that is more like a dream than reality. A person is always forgetting—which means dying. It is forgetfulness that is death, but it happens so slowly that a person doesn't feel much pain. It may be pain that a man most dreads in dying, but he often suffers a great deal more pain in mid life—even though he is in no danger of dying.'

No, Andri could not get away from Howard. He held him fast with his words, so confidential and so unlike him.

'When are you going to leave?'

'I think I can resign at any time because Julius could take over from me with no warning. Now he will have the job that many people thought he was cheated out of—and he deserves it.'

Suddenly they saw something among the lava boulders. Howard went closer and bent down.

'They are golden plovers,' he said.

One lay barely moving on the ground. The other tried to get away, but Howard caught it quickly. He lifted them both up to his chest and examined their burns. Their feet were burned, but the one in worst shape was burned on the breast, all the way to bloody flesh. It was mortally wounded. Howard had Andri hold the one with a chance of living while with a quick movement of the hand he broke the other one's neck.

'Lift it to flight,' he said to Andri, 'I expect it can survive, although it will limp for a few weeks.'

Andri released the bird and it flew away from them over the lava with a cheerful whistling. They saw it head in the direction of the mainland in the distance beyond the sea.

'We should bury the other one here in the ash,' said Howard.

They dug a small hole with their hands. Andri was bare-handed, but Howard had on thick leather gloves.

'It will soon be roasted here,' said Andri as they stood up.

They looked around. The land was more or less blending into a single lead-grey whole in the diminishing daylight after the sun had sunk into the sea.

Howard thought there must be more plovers in the vicinity, but it was hard to spot small birds in the twilight. Here and there glowing little streams of lava sent heat a long way out, and the ground around them was unreliable. Howard used his walking stick with an iron tip to see where it was safe to walk. But they didn't find any more birds and decided to turn back. The search for birds had led them much further down on the other side of the mountain than they had intended to go. It had become dark and the way back up the ridge risky, so they had to make several detours to get past embers which they could spot more easily now in the dense even twilight that had fallen.

Howard probed with his stick but it was slow going. In the lava the fresh breeze was growing more insistent, and when they looked back they saw the outlines of whitecaps on the dark surface of the sea.

They were tired and sweaty. Despite the cold air, the lava gave off heat. In the twilight a single twinkling star appeared in the chilly spring sky.

Suddenly the crater broke the silence, growling and rumbling as it gushed cinders and pumice dust. They took to their heels and got out from the shower of ashes. A glimmer of fire broke through the black cloud of soot. Andri lay down and listened to the hoarse voice of the volcano. He thought he heard Howard call, but the thunder drowned out other sounds. Then the squall subsided as suddenly as it had arisen.

Andri got to his feet and looked around, but he did not catch sight of Howard until he heard him call again—a call for help. What had happened? Andri hurried to him.

'Quick, grab the stick. . .the stick. . . .'

He saw Howard lying at full length beyond his reach, trying to raise his stick.

'Be careful,' called Howard, 'molten lava. . . .'

He raised his stick in Andri's direction, but it slipped from his hand before he could grasp it.

In the next breath Andri succeeded in grabbing Howard's shoulders and dragging him toward him out of the glowing lava which he could now see clearly.

He heard Howard make some kind of sound and breathe quickly. He was able to drag him up to shelter next to a lava boulder.

'Howard, Howard,' he called, but Howard had lost consciousness and lay with his mouth wide open and his eyes staring.

Andri called his name and tried to open his shirt collar, and then saw that one leg was nothing but a bloody lump and his trousers completely burned on the other leg.

It was clear to Andri that he had to get him to the hospital immediately if there was any hope of saving his life.

He tried to lift Howard up and carry him, but he was very heavy and the way difficult up the ridge in the dark.

There was nothing else to do but struggle. Every now and then he stopped to catch his breath. Howard had not regained consciousness, and it was extremely difficult to get a grip on him in such bad shape. After three attempts he lay Howard down and tried to call him back to consciousness, but he did not answer, his eyes staring out into the empty dark sky, with a blinking star and no sound but the moan of the breeze, for the thunder was no longer to be heard in the crater.

Andri continued to struggle up the ridge with Howard on his shoulders. It seemed that he got heavier with every step and the path more difficult. Finally he was completely exhausted and decided to leave Howard behind and run for help. Otherwise it would be too slow getting him to the hospital.

He put Howard down against a boulder and tried to memorize landmarks around him. It was hard to get his bearings in the landscape in the dark. Then he started running the last short distance up to the top of the ridge and did not stop before he got to the hospital, which was open.

The young doctor on night duty had been lying down and could not at first grasp what Andri was saying, or rather yelling, about what happened. But then right away he called the rescue squad, with a stretcher and other emergency equipment, and they dashed off, with Andri leading the way.

They had spotlights which lit up the area, but they were no help to Andri in locating himself, and they had to be turned off while he tried to get his bearings in relation to where he had left Howard.

Still, they found him quickly, and it seemed to Andri as if Howard had been able on his own to crawl a little distance up the ridge, but naturally that could not have happened. Besides, Howard was in exactly the same position he had been in when Andri left him, and he had not regained consciousness. The doctor examined him and shined his flashlight into his eyes, and they used time tending to his wounds that Andri thought could have been better spent hurrying with the man on the stretcher.

The young doctor finished his examination, stood up and said tonelessly, 'He has no vital signs.' Andri noticed for the first time that the young doctor was in his bedroom slippers.

A new day had begun to dawn, a glow over the white rims of the glaciers and the surface of the sea, smooth and ice blue.

Andri followed along after the men like a pack-train boy who does not know the journey's destination.

*

The sun shone through the window of the bookstore, where Andri lay inside half dressed, dozing and trying to flee reality and the waking facts with the help of a drug that the young doctor had administered to him and had given him to take home with him.

In the store windows there were none of the books that had been displayed just before the eruption, only a few yellowed newspapers and wrapping paper scattered about. Enormous fish flies were thriving there, buzzing blissfully up into the sunshine in the window and then back into the half-darkened room where Andri had lain slumbering for several days. Left-over food and dirty dishes sat on the table in front of him with the coffee pot, cups and little tubs for pills that had been scattered around the table with sugar and cigarette butts.

Why hadn't Sara come?

Why had he given in to the visions and fantasy of dreams rather than get up and look straight in the eye of events that could not be altered?

Suddenly a man was sitting in front of him whose presence startled him and whom at first he thought to be a hallu-cination, one of those ominous wandering troop who had filled his room and the shop and had come at him with weird behaviour and stupidity. At one point he thought it was the group of Danish fashion people who had held a show in the half-buried cemetery.

But then this man he knew well, the sergeant at the police station and no fashion model, a good reliable man whom he had known for a long time.

'There is a coffee pot somewhere there. I've probably used up all the coffee—and sugar in the bowl if the flies haven't devoured it to the last grain.'

But the sergeant did not want to brew coffee and the flies continued to have their sugar undisturbed.

What was the man talking about?

Oh yes, he was reviewing the night, the walk in search of birds, the accident, coming to the hospital.

'Yes, I talked to you the first time at the hospital, after they gave you a shot. . . .'

'These birds?' asked the sergeant.

'We found two plovers.'

'Two plovers?'

'They weren't able to fly. We buried one, the other one flew out of my hand when I let it go. Doesn't it say somewhere that not a sparrow falls to earth against the will of the Lord?'

'Yes, it certainly does.'

The sergeant rubbed his high forehead while he closed his eyes, as though he were going over something in his mind. Maybe he was praying? He had a wide worn wedding ring on his right hand.

'And then you turned back?' he said finally.

'Soon afterwards.'

'Why couldn't they fly, the plovers?'

'They had had a shock.'

'A shock?'

The sergeant looked at Andri without asking anything further.

'Are you interrogating me?' Andri asked after some moments of silence, during which nothing could be heard but the buzzing of the flies, which came in a wide curve out of the shop to the sugar delicacy on the table.

'No, no, but I couldn't get a complete report from you the other night.'

'You don't believe then that I am in any way to blame?'

'Of course not, that hasn't crossed anyone's mind.'

'Are you sure about that?'

'It would be absurd. It was an accident, a tragic accident. Not a living soul has any doubt about it.'

They fell silent again.

Andri looked closely at the sergeant. It was apparent that the man spoke sincerely. And again they heard nothing but the buzzing of the flies.

'I don't hear any booming in the crater.'

'No, it has stopped.'

'The crater?'

'And there is no more lava flow.'

'Since when?'

'Since the other night. That was probably the last spurt, which fell on you.'

'What time was that?'

'Four minutes to twelve, the geologists say.'

'Four minutes. It is exactly four minutes that scientists say mankind has left to live.'

'They have passed.'

'Four minutes left, if the whole life of mankind was one day, say the scientists, who are always warning us, and no one pays attention. The clock still reads four minutes to twelve.'

'It's remarkable,' said the sergeant, 'that the lava flow seems to have stopped in exactly the same area it did five or six thousand years ago.'

'Was our whole effort for nothing then?'

'No, the seawater cooling probably prevented the harbour entrance from being closed and several hundred tons of lava from going into the harbour. The old rock layer shows where the lava stopped five or six thousand years ago.'

'And is that at the same place as now?'

The sergeant nodded his head.

The flies were still moving about. Andri swung his hand at them and tried to shoo them away, but then they lit on a picked and shrivelled smoked leg of lamb that was lying uncovered in a bowl in the corner, on a mound of books.

'What time is it?' he asked the sergeant.

The sergeant looked at his wrist watch. He had a light-blue letter tattooed on the back of his hand so that he would be identified if his body were found washed up on the shore.

'It's just after three.'

Andri set his watch, which had stopped. He hadn't wound it since the accident.

The sergeant went to the door.

'Is there anything I can do for you?' he asked.

'No, I don't think so.'

He wanted to ask the sergeant about Sara. Who would have gone to her? Probably the minister. It was difficult to imagine Sara listening to words of consolation from the minister, and yet—?

But he did not ask anything. It would not have been any use. He listened to the sergeant go out of the shop and out onto the black street outside, where the sunshine streamed as it had the previous days. Only one thing was clear to him: he would not postpone any longer going to Sara and facing her. Would her eyes be full of tears or would she laugh, as the women in the sagas did when their grief was the most intense?

He felt his anxiety growing from a lump in his chest until it held him by the throat.

Why had he not gone straight to her the other night—had jealousy prevented it? Self accusation?

And the eruption stopped at exactly the moment Howard had become its victim.

Was that not an uncanny coincidence?

*

On the way to Sara's he continuously went over in his mind what he would say to her. Much hinged on the first words: I am sorry that I haven't come sooner, but I have not been myself. . . or, I have blamed myself so much for not having prevented it, for our having gone that way—no it was not he who had led the walk, it was Howard. And now Howard was out of the story, and he did not have to be afraid of him on her account, no longer needed to dread their night games in the Consul's house.

If Sara was thinking along those lines, what then could he say?

Every word could become an accusation of himself if it were not used correctly. Maybe it would be better in that case to remain silent. . . ?

There was the house, its white walls grown mottled grey from rain and storms.

Now there was sunshine, endless sunshine with the breeze from the north, and the house seemed to have sunk several inches into the ground, the roof like hands in prayer. What kind of delusion was he having? Didn't he see springtime everywhere about him, vegetation that was waking to life? In the cracks of the pavement dark green tooth-edged dandelion leaves had begun spreading out, and yellow dandelions would be laughing in the sun in a few days.

He hesitated a moment on the walk by the steps and looked in the windows to see whether a face might be observing him, but they were dark and empty.

The front door stood half open, and when he went up the steps he heard talking inside. It was a man talking on the phone. But what?—didn't the voice he heard sound familiar? Yes, there could not be any mistake about it, it was none other than Kalli talking on the phone. What could he be doing here? Maybe something in connection with packing?

Andri slipped into the entrance hall. The door was open into the office where Kalli stood at the telephone, but he had his back turned to Andri and was not yet aware of him. Then through the open doorway he noticed Sara sitting in a chair in the living room with suitcases on the floor.

Apparently she was leaving for Reykjavik. Howard would

probably be buried there.

She was wearing a black turtle-neck sweater with rolled up sleeves and her arms were bruised and bloody.

She watched Andri come in without showing any change in expression or saying a word. There was smoke in the air.

'Sara,' he stammered, 'Sara, I couldn't come before this, I couldn't.'

He tried to smile, but it only felt like a grimace.

She sat with a pipe between her hands and looked at him as if he were an object or a peculiar animal. How long and thin her neck had suddenly become and how small her head.

'Do you want a smoke?' she said. 'We have some hashish.'

'No thanks, I am half-numb from drugs,' he answered and felt how furry and thick his tongue was, as if he could scarcely bring it forward in his mouth.

'I know I should have come over right away that night, but I wasn't in my right mind. I was full of drugs and living in a dream world. I wasn't aware of the passage of time.'

'I told her that,' a voice said from behind him. It was Kalli.

'You?' Kalli stood in the doorway, but Andri did not turn toward him.

'Yes, I came over as soon as I heard.'

Sara scratched her arms as if she had eczema.

'The other night?' asked Andri, barely able to get the words out.

'Yes, the other night. We boys were playing poker in the cafeteria when we heard about it. They had brought him to the hospital then. I saw Howard on the examining table with the doctor.' Andri stared at him.

'I knocked on the door until they came,' Kalli continued his story. He was bare-headed, his Che Guevara cap lying on the table next to the suitcases.

'I was lying awake,' said Sara, dragging deeply on the pipe. 'I knew that something would happen. . . .'

'My brother Gubbi is going to drive us up to the airport,' Kalli said, 'he will be coming in a couple of minutes.'

'You and Sara?' Andri cried out.

'Her name isn't Sara any longer,' Kalli answered and took a drag from her pipe. She started scratching her arms again.

'She has another name now,' Kalli smirked.

'What have you done to your hair,' Andri shouted, and his tongue had now suddenly become long and smooth. 'You cut it. . . .'

'Don't you think it's just right for her?' Kalli answered. Sara grinned broadly, her face disfigured.

'What have you done to your hair?'

'I gave it to Howard,' she answered and the smile left her face. Her countenance became hard and white, her nose sharp, and her mouth long and thin. . . .

'She is in the old style of the Weimar Republic, before the Nazis destroyed it.'

Her hair was in uneven layers as though she had done it herself without a mirror, very high up on the nape of the neck, just like an old-fashioned boy's haircut.

'I cut it and put it in the coffin with him,' she said gruffly.

'Her name is now Grima,' Kalli said triumphantly. 'It has a triple meaning. In the first place, it means "night", and in the second place it means "mask". And now she has to live up to it when we become masked men and urban guerillas in West Germany.'

'Urban guerillas! What stupidity.'

'Don't you think she could be one of the Bader-Meinhoff Group?' Kalli asked, and put his beret on her head.

Sara tried to smile with the hat on her head.

'It's absurd,' Andri objected, 'it's nothing but a farce.'

'Of course, didn't you know that before this?' answered Sara. 'Everything is a farce.'

'But this is mental cruelty. You can't allow yourself to be

200

treated this way, Sara.'

'Worry more about yourself,' she answered in a poisonous tone.

She looked at him between thin slits in her eyes as if from a gun turret. 'Who are you?' she asked him, every word hitting him like a shot from ambush, 'star dust, hydrogen that dissolves. . . ?'

Kalli laughed, 'Yes, she knows the story of creation.'

The pipe was finished and he knocked the ashes out into an ashtray and put it in his pocket.

'Sara, be on your guard against Kalli, he just wants to use you.'

'And you don't?' Kalli answered sarcastically.

'What are you talking about?' Sara asked. She rubbed her arms and stared at the red scratches.

'Have you heard people mention a girl called Vala? He treated her badly, and he let us boys watch what he did with her.'

'So you are an accessory,' Kalli said and laughed. 'All spectators are accessories.'

'We have grown tired of being in a rut here,' he went on. 'No, we're going to where something is happening. Western Europe is collapsing because it doesn't want to live, because it has used up its vitality. You know, people jumped overboard on the *Titanic* with their pockets full of gold bars, and sank straight to the bottom.'

Sara was standing up.

'Sara, you have to talk to me. You have to talk to me seriously.'

But she did not seem to pay any attention to his words.

'Just two minutes,' he asked, 'you have to, you can't deny me that.'

Kalli had finished locking the suitcases.

'You will regret later going with him. Bad luck follows him.'

201

'And what follows you?' she asked, grimacing in an unsuccessful attempt to smile.

'Sara, I ask you, for the last time, I ask you to give me a chance. I ask you in the name of everything we have had together in the past and which I thought meant something to you.'

Kalli laughed loudly. 'You are just like an old movie from the days of Rudolph Valentino.'

Sara also tried to laugh, but then turned away from Andri and began putting the leather straps around the suitcases that Kalli had closed.

'Has Kalli given you back the knife that he took away from Rikki?' Andri blurted out. 'Has he done that?'

They both looked questioningly at Andri.

'What are you talking about?' Sara asked.

'You took the knife away from Rikki when you were fighting,' Andri repeated, and watched Sara to see her reaction.

'Sara and everyone else knows that I never took a knife from him. We traded knives and that was all there was to it. You know that as well as I do.'

'That happened once in another life—or a bad dream,' she said and kept on fastening the straps.

'Sara,' Andri begged, 'you can't ever think that I am at all to blame for what happened.'

'She saw you spying on them the other day,' Kalli said.

'I couldn't prevent it.'

'That you spied on them?'

'I didn't do that, but I was talking about not being able to prevent Howard's going out on the lava. I wasn't with him then, you have to believe me. He went down onto the crust. It is easy to suspect a person when he is the only one left to tell the tale, just like when Rikki fell and Kalli was the only one with him and had the knife on him.'

All at once it was as though she came back to life and looked in his face. 'I loved Howard. I was going with him to America—it was all set. And now I am going in a completely different direction. Everything is going in a different direction.'

Andri thought, she's not telling the truth, she is only tormenting me. She is always saying things about herself that cannot be true.

A car had stopped outside the gate with the engine idling.

'Gubbi is here,' Kalli called and took one of his suitcases in each hand.

Sara was going to take the third bag, but Andri stopped her.

'Don't go. Don't go with Kalli, I beg you—because I. . . because I. . . because you cannot, because I . . . .' The words stuck in his throat.

'Yes, it's what must now happen as things have turned out,' she pushed him roughly away from her, took the bag and hurried out of the house with it. Gubbi had got out of the car and out on the pavement he took the suitcase from her and put it into the trunk.

Kalli ran back to the house and up the steps where Andri stood looking at them, the sunshine in his face, unshaved, in a jacket and blue jeans.

'I just want to shake your hand for the poem,' he said and put out his hand. But Andri did not take it.

'I haven't written a poem recently.'

'Oh yes, you have, but you made it out of something much hotter than before, and now I know you are a better poet than Grimur the lighthouse keeper despite everything, and maybe a greater revolutionary too, acting without hesitation.'

Kalli grabbed Andri tightly around the shoulder and pulled him toward him without Andri's having time to resist, then he ran back down the pavement to the car, where Sara was sliding in, black and slim with a beret and shiny boots.

What was the third thing concealed in her name?

Kalli plunked himself into the back seat next to her and

203

slammed the car door, the sun gleaming on the hood.

Gubbi started the car moving. He lifted his right hand from the steering wheel and waved to Andri, who did not return it.

A little dust swirled up from the car when it turned to go up the ridge toward the airport.

Behind him Andri heard footsteps and knew it was old Ella moving about.

He waited for her to say something and then he could turn around, but she made no sound other than slamming the heavy oak door.

Andri looked over his shoulder and saw the warped and windblown front door with carved dragons and the year written in Roman numerals.

Then he went slowly down the steps. The car had disappeared on its way up to the airport, but in the crumbling pavement the shapes were forming of dandelions that were just to the point of opening out laughing into the cold sunshine.

*

Andri went back into town along the wharf.

A transport ship was tied up in front of the freezing plant. Julius came up to him smiling and said that he had been to get a directive from the town authorities to stop the loading which had been ordered earlier of all the heavy machines and equipment. They began talking.

Julius said that the geologists believed the eruption was more or less over—no noticeable lava flow or ash fall, and the cloud of smoke from the crater had disappeared. The lava now covered twenty square kilometres of land where before there had been sea up to seventy metres deep. The harbour was deep enough for large ships and the lava flow had now created one of the most protected harbours in the country, so that natural catastrophes had not just produced destruction and loss. And also the community had become more famous and would bring more tourists to see it in the future.

He and Julius went along the high edge of lava that had swallowed up buildings along the harbour and obliquely up the road that had been laid for the twelve-inch steel pipes and high-pressure pumps, which stood ready like cannons to meet the advance of the lava if it should begin anew. But there was no movement apparent.

Bulldozers and steamrollers had smoothed out the deposits of pumice over a large area that had been seeded with oats and fescue. Flocks of gulls and kittiwakes were scattered over the pumice fields.

'We won't be seeing much grass,' said Andri, 'if the gulls gobble up all the seed.'

'Oh yes, it won't hurt anything,' Julius answered, 'it all comes back out of them and then has an even better chance of germinating than before.'

He laughed so that a wide space showed between his front teeth, as if he were missing a tooth.

They walked up to a geologist who had a measuring device on a tripod out on the lava field. He told them it was now possible to see down into the central bowl of the volcano crater and that it would not be too long before they could go down into it on ropes for closer examination.

When they came back down from the lava field they saw a fishing boat appear at the furthest edge of the harbour entrance with people up on deck. Birds hovered along the stone cliffs performing all kinds of stunts in the air, and the happy shouts of children with their mothers could be heard on board the boat.

'There are the people coming back,' Julius said, 'and it won't be long before the tiled rooms in the freezing plant are full of girls again, packing fish fillets in paper boxes that smell of cleanliness like a chemist's shop.'

Andri nodded his head.

'I hope you will not be leaving us,' said Julius.

205

'Well, I had planned to go,' Andri answered, 'but now I'll probably stay.'

'Excellent, fine, you can choose whatever work you want, you are one of us. . . .'

'And yet I never felt, as I do now, that I was coming here from somewhere else.'

'What foolishness,' Julius shook his hand.

'You can have my old manager's job, I know you have a good way with people—and you would do well.'

'Well, I'm not so sure about that. . . .'

'Oh yes, it couldn't be otherwise. I can see it in you.'

They had got out to the harbour wall. The guillemots circled in agile games of courtship while the fulmars whinnied and laughed above them in the clear air.

'A person thinks that he lives somewhere,' Andri continued, 'and then all of a sudden everything seems foreign to him and he becomes an outsider.'

Julius waved to the people coming on the boat into the channel by the harbour light.

'What were you saying?' Julius asked.

'It was nothing.'

'Yes, of course we are all outsiders compared with these birds who have been here since the islands rose from the sea,' Julius said.

The people in the boat waved at them energetically, whistled and laughed.

'And the people there are coming home. They aren't outsiders.'

'Yes,' Andri answered, 'they are lucky, they are like the guillemots and fulmars.'